"Peyton," Matt said, her name a stiff, stern greeting.

She stood there, her coat unbuttoned and splotched from the rain, a Christmas plaid scarf hanging listlessly from her collar. She appeared pale, hesitant, as if she'd rather be anywhere else. The sudden unwitting thrill of seeing her so unexpectedly faded as her eyes met his and her expression turned distant and cool. He missed the fire of her arguments, the zeal she'd thrown at him for no better reason than she enjoyed their debates. But since the night at the beach house, she'd avoided him.

"Matt," she returned evenly, waiting in the doorway of his office for an invitation she seemed to know he didn't want to extend. "Do you have a minute?"

"Actually, no." He glanced at his watch. "I'm due in Providence in an hour and should already be on my way. Why don't you talk to Jessica about whatever's on your mind and she can fill me in later."

"I could do that, but I don't really think you want her to be the first to know that we're…"

The unuttered word slammed into him. A sucker punch. "Come in," he told her. "Close the door."

THE MATCHMAKER'S PLAN

Karen Toller Whittenburg

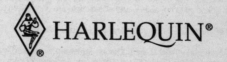

HARLEQUIN®

TORONTO • NEW YORK • LONDON
AMSTERDAM • PARIS • SYDNEY • HAMBURG
STOCKHOLM • ATHENS • TOKYO • MILAN • MADRID
PRAGUE • WARSAW • BUDAPEST • AUCKLAND

ISBN 0-373-75018-8

THE MATCHMAKER'S PLAN

Copyright © 2004 by Karen Whittenburg Crane.

ABOUT THE AUTHOR

Karen Toller Whittenburg credits her love of reading with inspiring her writing career. She enjoys fiction in every form, but romance continues to hold a special place for her. As a teenager she spent long, lovely hours falling in love with Emilie Loring's heroines, falling in love with every hero and participating in every adventure. It's no wonder she always dreamed of being a romance writer. Karen lives in Oklahoma and divides her time between writing and running a household, both full-time and fulfilling careers.

Books by Karen Toller Whittenburg

HARLEQUIN AMERICAN ROMANCE

†The Texas Sheikhs
*The Billion-Dollar Braddocks
††Matchmaker, Matchmaker

Don't miss any of our special offers. Write to us at the following address for information on our newest releases.

Harlequin Reader Service
U.S.: 3010 Walden Ave., P.O. Box 1325, Buffalo, NY 14269
Canadian: P.O. Box 609, Fort Erie, Ont. L2A 5X3

MEMO

TO: Jessica Martin-Kingsley
Staff Supervisor and Volunteer Liaison

FROM: Matthew Danville
CEO, Danville Foundation

SUBJECT: Confidential

Jessica—
In regard to your latest memo to me, referencing Peyton O'Reilly and next spring's Black-and-White Ball charity event, let me remind you that Ms. O'Reilly is a volunteer and cannot be reprimanded for (as you phrased it) "…irritating the oysters out of everyone with whom she comes into contact."

As I'm sure you recall, she was put in charge of the B&W fund-raiser at your suggestion and despite my (and a few other board

members') reservations about allowing someone so new to take charge of such an important
fund-raising event. However, Ms. O'Reilly
was eager to take on the challenge, cam-
paigned enthusiastically for the task, and was
approved (on a vote of 5–4) as the B&W event
chairperson. As she has (to date) done nothing
either unethical or illegal, I see no recourse but
to allow her to continue in this voluntary position.

In future, perhaps you will see the wisdom
of giving new volunteers ample time to dem-
onstrate the full extent of their *irritation factor*
before putting them in a position from which
they can (for several long months) drive our
oysters insane.

Chapter One

There was ample reason for Matthew Danville to be having a fabulous time.

Ainsley, his baby sister, had just been married in a beautiful ceremony; his best friend, Dr. Ivan Donovan, had just become his brother-in-law; the reception—planned perfectly to the nth degree by his other sister, Miranda—was off to a rollicking good start; his parents, Charles and Linney, were home for the occasion and focused—for once—on the happiness of their children. Everything was just as it should be in the world of the Danvilles.

And that's the way he kept trying to think of it.

Even if there was no escaping the reality that Ainsley was married, Miranda was engaged, and the world Matt had always counted on was changing.

In a few hours, Ainsley would leave with Ivan for a two-week honeymoon in Italy, and when she returned, it wouldn't be to Danfair. She'd be living in

Providence with Ivan. She'd call another place home, and when she came to Danfair, it would be only as a visitor. A few hours here or there. Possibly an overnight on special occasions. But then she'd leave again, returning to her own home. Not far from Newport and the famous cliffs, mile-wise, but still a whole other life away. Matt couldn't quite get his mind around that.

Home without Ainsley.

Miranda would marry Nate Shepard and leave, too. She was newly engaged and no wedding date had been set as yet—at least as far as Matt knew—but he didn't think it would be long. Probably by spring, Danfair would be home only to him and Andrew, Ainsley's twin, born an hour before her. A place where two brothers, both bachelors, slept and ate and kept their clothes. They'd manage just fine, of course. There would always be other people around; a rotating staff of immigrants and foreign students sponsored by the Danville Foundation was a fixture at Danfair. A fairly constant stream of gardeners, landscapers and maintenance crews were on the estate at any given moment, as well. And guests. Miranda and Ainsley would no doubt visit frequently, if for no better reason than to make sure he and Andrew adequately missed them.

But it wouldn't be the same. The magnificent mansion that had been both refuge and playground, shelter and security for the four of them growing up would become strangely quiet and empty.

With the girls married and all of them well into adulthood, Matt suspected his parents might curtail their occasional visits home to Danfair to once or twice a year. Over the course of his life, he'd seen them spend less and less time in the States and more and more in other countries, fulfilling their mission of philanthropy. They carried out the work of the Foundation, whatever the personal cost, offering help and hope to children of other cultures while leaving their own children to grow up—for the most part—on their own. Charles and Linney's extended absences had turned their offspring into virtual orphans, supervised but not parented, protected but not policed. It had made for a strange sort of freedom, a childhood Matt had always considered a rather extraordinary gift. The four of them had formed an odd little family of children and had turned their home into a playhouse where they'd lived, quite happily, without much adult interference.

Matt was proud to take his share of credit for the fact that they'd all turned out to be good, upstanding citizens. It had been his responsibility, after all, to set the example. He couldn't remember a time he hadn't been conscious of being the oldest, the pathfinder, the first in a new generation of Danvilles. He was the firstborn son of the firstborn son and he'd been given the name Jonathan, as had all firstborn sons before him. The middle name varied from one generation to the next. His happened to be Matthew, his father's was Charles. But it was the inherited "Jonathan" that designated him as the one who would continue the work of the family foundation. He'd been born to responsibility, to be the role model not only for his younger brother and sisters, but for his cousins and for the next generation, too. It wasn't a job he'd applied for or particularly wanted, but it was his job, nonetheless.

"I'm thinking of sending you a memo," the pretty woman in his arms said with a laugh. "If only to get your attention."

And Matt returned to the pleasure at hand—dancing with Jessica Martin-Kingsley. "You already have my attention, Jessica." Which was true enough. She was a woman accustomed to getting whatever she wanted—the only child of wealthy parents who doted on her and made generous donations to the Danville Foundation at her request, Jessica was both a tremendous asset to the work of the Foundation and an attractive nuisance—and it was becoming transparently apparent that she wanted Matt, even though she was not only not what he wanted, but married besides. "There probably isn't a man in the room who wouldn't love to be in my place at this very moment. Including your husband.''

Her smile was one of pretty calculation. ''You're a gentleman, Matthew.'' She always called him Matthew, never Matt. ''A liar, but a gentleman. Your attention has wandered ever since this evening began—I've been watching you—and if I can't distract you, then there must be something momentous on your mind. Please tell me you're not still worrying about the Black-and-White Ball. I feel just awful about that entire situation.''

So did he, but he wasn't about to soothe her conscience over it. ''Why would I be worried?'' He turned her expertly, smiled as if he hadn't a care in the world. ''Especially tonight when my thoughts are a very long way from anything having to do with the Foundation.''

Her laughter was softly acerbic. ''Your thoughts are never far from the Foundation, Matthew. Whatever you may pretend.''

He caught a shimmer of white in his peripheral vision a second before his elbow was bumped once and then—lest he think it an accident—again. Baby to his rescue.

''Oops!'' Ainsley said brightly. ''Guess I wasn't looking where we were going.'' Her smile encompassed Jessica, Matt and her own current dance partner, their cousin, Scott. ''Matt! What a happy coincidence. You're just the brother I wanted to dance with next.'' And as smooth as cream, she negotiated a change of partners. Scott swept Jessica away before she quite realized the old switcheroo, and Matt was left holding the bride.

''Nicely done, Baby,'' he said, using her nickname and knowing how very much he would miss his little sister. ''Were you worried that I couldn't stave off Ms. Martin-Kingsley's advances all by myself?''

Ainsley, gorgeous in her splashy beaded silk wedding gown, radiant in her happiness, gave him an arch look. ''I knew you could. I was worried you wouldn't. Big difference. But mainly I wanted to dance with my big brother.''

Matt took that at face value, although she had already danced with him twice. Knowing Ainsley, he suspected there was another explanation, a hidden agenda which would be revealed in a minute or two if he simply waited her out. Or if he asked pertinent questions. It didn't really matter which course he chose, because Ainsley was never especially good at keeping her own counsel. ''Are you having a good time?'' he asked, knowing the answer, wanting only to see her face light up with it again.

''Best time ever,'' she replied, dimples framing her smile. ''But ask me tomorrow. The wedding night might turn out to be the best time I've ever had. Then again, the honeymoon is going to last two whole weeks and *that* could be the best. And after that, I get to live with Ivan and sleep with him every night and *that* could be the absolute best time ever. You never know.''

''More information than a brother needs…except for the fact that you're happy. Ivan had better make sure you stay that way.''

''He makes me happy just by breathing,'' she said, and the conviction in her voice made Matt almost envious.

He gave her a hug and began moving toward the edge of the dance floor as the song neared its conclusion, but Ainsley, in a clever countermove, managed to alter their direction and bumped him, a little forcefully, into another tuxedoed back. Her devious plan, Matt thought, was revealed. He'd suspected for some time that Ainsley, a matchmaker's apprentice with two successful matches under her belt, had a specific someone in mind for him and had been trying to find a good opportunity to set him up with what she referred to as an *introduction of possibilities.* And here was the proof, standing right in front of him when he turned around. Peyton O'Reilly, possibly the most *impossible* woman of his acquaintance.

''Oops!'' Ainsley said brightly, but this time her smile encircled only one. ''Ivan! What a happy coincidence! You're exactly the husband I wanted to dance with next.''

Somehow, in the lull between the end of one song and the start of another, Ainsley pulled another switcheroo and danced off with her new husband, giving Matt a little wave of encouragement and leaving him with two unappealing options. Walk away from Peyton or stay and dance with her. He didn't want to do the latter but, as Jessica had accused, he was a gentleman. A liar, perhaps, on occasion. But still a gentleman. ''Peyton,'' he said with a polished warmth, ''you look lovely tonight. Thank you for coming.''

Her smile was equally noncommittal. ''Thank you for the invitation.''

An invitation, she knew, of course, hadn't come from him. She and Ainsley were friends, worked together as volunteers at the new pediatric center. She knew, too—or believed she knew, at any rate—that if the decision had been left to him, she wouldn't have received an invitation to the wedding at all. From the moment they'd met, Matt had somehow managed to rub Ms. O'Reilly the wrong way. And vice versa. But Ainsley refused to believe the two of them couldn't be friends, that the sparks between them weren't indicative of romantic possibilities, and Matt felt certain that was why she'd arranged this devious and awkward introduction of possibilities moment on the dance floor. Consequently, here he stood, face-to-face with Peyton, friction already established in the course of two overly polite sentences and not a possibility of rescue in sight. But this was Ainsley's wedding reception. A happy occasion. He could spend ten minutes being nice to Peyton O'Reilly.

"Dance with me?" he asked, because it seemed the obvious thing to say. "This is my favorite song."

Her eyebrows went up. The corners of her mouth lifted. And his lips moved upward in unbidden response. Which seemed the effect she consistently had on him. One minute she was the most exasperating, irritating woman he knew, and the next minute he got all tangled up in her smile. Peyton wasn't a particularly beautiful woman, but there was something about her long, dusky hair, not quite black, not entirely brown, that made a man think it would feel thick and luxurious tangled in his hands. There was a trusting innocence in her hazel eyes that had a man standing taller before he even knew why. And her smile, as wide and warm and winsome as an early spring, got under a man's skin before he could recall exactly why he was upset with her.

"Well, then," she said in that soft Louisiana drawl that played so charmingly against the clipped

New England accents all around them. "If it's your *favorite* song, I don't see how I can refuse."

She moved into his arms easily and fit there as if she belonged. Which surprised him. He'd thought—if he'd thought about it at all—that the two of them, in close quarters, would be all odd angles and awkward adjustments, their bodies at the same cross-purpose as their personalities. Instead, it felt effortless to hold her, and more pleasurable than he would ever have imagined. She smelled fresh, clean, as if she'd been dipped in dew and dried in the morning sun. Her body swayed against his—not too close, but close enough—and he was aware—very aware—of her curvy, womanly physique. This was no pencil-thin, reed-slim female he held. Peyton was full breasted and nicely filled out, and if not exactly voluptuous, she was certainly well proportioned. A subtle and seductive response welled inside him and Matt reluctantly recognized it for what it was—sexual attraction. A sizzle beneath the surface. A spark waiting to be struck.

Okay, so he would give Ainsley credit for having picked up on something he'd missed. But this spark of attraction was going nowhere. He didn't especially want to set himself ablaze, for one thing, and even if he did, he felt certain Peyton would stomp the spark out before it ever had a chance to catch fire.

"I'm really going to miss working with Ainsley at the pediatric center," she said, destroying his moment of fantasy with her stilted, studied remark.

"She's only going to Italy for two weeks, you know. She will be back."

"Well, yes, but it won't be the same, will it?"

He drew back slightly, kept dancing as he frowned down at her. "Because she's married?"

Peyton blinked, then she laughed. Just a little gurgle of amusement in her throat, but still a laugh that wrapped its warmth around him like the hug of an old friend. "No," she replied, drawing the syllable out long and low. "Because she won't be volunteering at the center anymore."

This was news to him. "Why not?"

"What she told me is that she's getting so many clients, she has to curtail some of her volunteer hours."

"Clients?" He repeated before he thought. "She has too many *clients?*"

Peyton drew back, returned his frown. "What? You didn't think she was good at her job?"

"Ainsley is a match..." He bit back the rest of the word with a snap. He didn't go around telling people his sister was a matchmaker's apprentice, that she actually believed she could kindle romance simply by putting two people in proximity and waiting for the possibilities to erupt. Luckily, Ainsley didn't go around telling people, either. Ilsa Fairchild Braddock, the founder of IF Enterprises, an elite matchmaking service, was wise enough—thank goodness—to insist upon discretion. Except, of course, that discretion had never been Ainsley's strong suit and there seemed to be quite a number of people who knew that IF Enterprises had more to do with personal relationships than public relations. Still, he found himself hoping, rather fervently, that Peyton wasn't privy to that particular information, that she didn't suspect Ainsley wanted to set up a match between the two of them. "Ainsley is a match for whatever she sets her mind to," he said, correcting his slip of the tongue. "I'm just a little surprised she told you she would be doing less volunteering before she told me."

He saw the warmth recede in her eyes, knew he'd offended her in some inexplicable and mysterious way.

"Ainsley's been a good friend to me ever since I moved to Rhode Island earlier this year," Peyton explained in a stiffly neutral tone. "We talk about a lot of things and I'm absolutely certain she didn't intend for you to feel slighted because she told me before she told you."

"I don't feel *slighted*. Only a little surprised, that's all."

"Oh, perhaps I misunderstood."

It was clear from her tone she didn't think so, and Matt had to wonder how his conversations with Peyton turned into these ridiculous and exaggerated attempts not to offend each other. Resulting in greater offense than if they'd either one meant to offend in the first place. "I'm sure she will tell me," he said. "When she thinks of it."

"Knowing Ainsley, I imagine she thinks she already told you."

Which was almost certainly true—Ainsley went through life like a sunbeam, making the world a brighter place wherever she happened to alight, blissfully unaware of practical matters—but somehow it annoyed him that Peyton knew his sister so well. "Perhaps she does," he answered, his voice sounding as stilted as hers.

For a moment—the space of five, maybe six heartbeats—Peyton drifted in his arms like a summer cloud, her steps perfectly matched to his, her body effortlessly responding to the slightest nuance of his lead. Matt marveled again at the graceful ease with which they danced together, wondered how the action could be so uncomplicated and their conversation so problematic.

"I met your mother and father." The sentence came out sounding a little desperate, as if she'd searched long and hard to think of something unexceptional to say. "They're remarkable people."

"Yes," he agreed. "They are."

"You must be so proud to be their son."

"Yes, I am." And that was about as far as that conversational line could go. He couldn't very well return the compliment, as he'd met her parents and found them unremarkable except for their great fascination with their new money and status. Peyton didn't seem to share their attitude, but then that was just an impression. Based on little more than observation and, of course, on frequent and somewhat heated exchanges of opinion about allowing her creative ideas—and she had many of them—to run full steam ahead, regardless of who or what got bulldozed along the way. Peyton demonstrated little patience for protocol and procedure, and a decided disdain for tradition. She believed fiercely—he knew this from painful experience—that raising the funding for a project was more important than coddling personalities, and she'd proved willing to butt heads with anyone who tried to derail her parade. *That* anyone being, lately and most often, him.

"Miranda did a great job of putting this event together," she ventured in her next conversational gambit. "What a great idea to have it here at the pediatric center so some of Dr. Donovan's patients could enjoy the celebration."

"Yes," he agreed, then deciding he could expend a little more effort, added, "Having the reception here was actually Ainsley's inspiration. Luckily, Miranda didn't murder her for changing her mind at the very last minute.''

The fact that he'd volunteered more than one syllable seemed to startle Peyton and she made no response. Matt felt frustrated with her and with the nagging pleasure he experienced being close to her and holding her in his arms. Since taking the reins of the Black-and-White Ball fund-raising committee, she'd caused him nothing but headaches. In his office, she found it easy to tackle his opinion that sometimes the long way around a problem was the right way. In committee meetings, she had no problem at all finding the words to challenge his position. But put the two of them together in a social setting and—*wham!*—nothing but uninspired sentences and stuttering attempts at conversation.

Where was the passion she waved like a red flag the very second he tried to advise or caution her? But even as the question crossed his mind, he knew. It was here, radiating between their bodies, conducting a conversation all its own, an uninvited guest who seemed intent on making a scene.

And, Matt realized suddenly, she was as aware of the underlying attraction and its accompanying tension as he was…and just as determined not to acknowledge it.

''I met Miranda's fiancé earlier,'' Peyton said in

yet another attempt to pretend she was unaware of any undertones. "His older set of twins attend the same private school as my sister, Scarlett. She's a little older than they are, I think."

Matt couldn't help himself. As he realized she was fighting an unwelcome attraction to him, he began to see everything about her in a new light. The spark Ainsley had recognized, and hoped to fan into a romantic blaze, was mutual and it explained a lot. Not the least being his instant and rather keen fascination with the sensual curve of her lips and the abrupt and rather defensive tilt of her chin.

He tried a smile, and immediately the sparkle leaped back into her eyes and the sizzle streaked through him, as startling as a lightning strike. *Interesting.* "Do you have any brothers? More than one sister?" he asked, as much to put a little distance between himself and those thoughts as to keep up his end of the conversation.

"No, just Scarlett. Some days she makes me wish I had at least one more sibling to help keep her corralled."

"Is 'keeping her corralled' your responsibility?"

Her gaze flashed up to his, flitted away. "My parents haven't always been...accessible. They worked many long hours at the restaurant before it turned into a franchise. The restaurant chain is one of those so-called overnight success stories that took years of hard work to make happen. Taking care of Scarlett sort of naturally fell to me.''

''We have that in common then.''

''What?''

''I took care of my younger siblings, too.''

''You did?''

He didn't think she needed to sound quite so astonished. ''I did.''

''Hmm.''

''*Hmm?* What does that mean?''

She moistened her lips, and it occurred to him she was, perhaps, a little intimidated. Which should have made him feel he had the advantage, but didn't. ''It doesn't mean anything,'' she answered, ''except, maybe, that you don't seem like the nurturing type.''

''What type do I seem like?''

Her smile flashed unexpectedly and the sizzle zapped him again. ''The type who likes to…''

But whatever she planned to say faded as something across the room caught and held her attention. She couldn't have glanced away for more than a second or two, but her tension was instantaneous and rippled from her body into his, and when her gaze returned to him, there was anger in her eyes.

''Matt,'' she said, ''I need your help. Please don't ask any questions, just play along with whatever I say. Please. I wouldn't ask you, except…''

Except he was the only hero handy. Intrigued, he

nodded. "You want to see if I'm the type of guy who will help a lady in distress."

She didn't offer even a frown in reply, just grabbed his hand and led him around and past the other couples on the dance floor, pausing briefly when they reached the edge. "This is probably going to sound insane to you, but it's the only way to deal with my mother. Please believe me."

If he'd been tempted to discount the seriousness of her request, her grip on his hand would have weighted it in her favor. He'd be lucky if he could wiggle his fingers tomorrow. Something had tipped her temper into the red, and the hesitant conversationalist of a few minutes ago had vanished, replaced by this woman with an agenda.

"Mother. Daddy." She greeted her parents in a tone delicate with respect, yet steely with impatience. "You know Matthew Danville, of course."

Rick O'Reilly, medium height, medium weight, over-the-top personality, was quick with a handshake, quicker with a smile. "Matt, good to see you, son. Great party. Good eats. Some pretty important guests, too." He waggled a pair of caterpillar eyebrows. "The wife's been trying to get up close and personal with that television-star fella. You know, the soap opera guy. Between us men, I don't see what he's got that we don't, but, hey, there's no understanding women to begin with. Know what I mean?''

''Richard, honestly…'' There was nothing medium or mediocre about Connie O'Reilly. If she had ever been her husband's counterpart, she'd since become splendidly sophisticated. Everything about her was studied and deliberate, stylish and expensive, gracious but somehow calculating. Matt couldn't decide if she expected him to shake her hand or kiss it. ''It was such a lovely wedding, Matthew. Rick and I are thrilled to have been invited.''

''We're thrilled you could come,'' he said, offering her not a handshake or a kiss on the hand, but his best the-Danville-Foundation-appreciates-your-contribution smile with a slight inclination of the head. Ainsley called the gesture his bow to the demigods who poured dollars into the work of the Foundation and expected royal treatment—at least—in return. The O'Reillys qualified on both counts. ''Celebrations would be meaningless without friends like you to share in our happiness.''

Which was neither true nor his personal opinion, but was what he said because he represented the Danville Foundation and because that's what people like the O'Reillys wanted to hear. He'd learned early that being a liar and a gentleman was his birthright, bought and paid for with stolen gold by his ancestor, Black Dan, the pirate. So Matt lied, and he did it well, because no one ever considered that his story might not be the truth.

"That's so sweet of you to say," Connie replied. "We've been simply overwhelmed at the warm welcome we've received here in Newport. Especially after hearing about that famous New England aloofness all these years."

"Aloofness-spoofness." Rick grinned broadly. "Y'all just promote that notion to keep out the riffraff. I've got your Yankee number."

"I believe you do." Matt felt a distinct liking for the older man and his what-you-see-is-what-you-get manners. It took a tough character to build a fortune with his bare hands, and Rick O'Reilly had earned the pride he wore as if it were the Congressional Medal of Honor. Matt envied him that privilege.

"I thought I saw Scarlett talking to you," Peyton said, her voice perfectly cordial, the grip she still had on Matt's hand distinctly impatient. "Did she leave?"

Mother and daughter exchanged a look long on subtext and riddled with tension, but painfully civil. "Yes, she did. Covington wanted to take her for a moonlight drive."

Peyton closed her eyes for a moment, took a slow breath. "And you gave her permission?"

"Well, of course," Connie answered, her Southern smile skimming Peyton to settle on Matt.

"Young people these days are always off on their own adventures, you know. And such a *nice* group of young men and women have included our Scarlett in their number. Richard and I were just talking about how easily she fits in here. But that's Scarlett for you, never meets a stranger."

"Did she leave in a group?" Peyton persisted. "Or just with him?"

Connie was clearly uncomfortable having this discussion in front of Matt. As, perhaps, Peyton had intended. "I trust Covington completely, Peyton. He's a lovely boy, as I'm sure Matthew would be happy to tell you."

Matt did not want to get in the middle of this. Not even a little.

As if sensing retreat, Peyton pressed her fingers hard into his, asking him to stay, even as she continued the visual wrestling match with her mother.

Connie didn't yield. "You know, Matthew, I would dearly love to meet Nick Shepard. If I promise not to be so gauche as to ask for his autograph, would you, perhaps, introduce me? I understand your sister, Miranda, is engaged to his brother. Won't that be nice, having a genuine celebrity in the family?"

A way out. A convenient segue from this family situation to less demanding company.

Matt was ready to take the opportunity offered,

but suddenly, Peyton was all smiles, her voice sifting accent and assent in a slow, sweet deception. "Oh, Mother, I did not bring Matthew over here so you could steal him away from me." Her smile shifted to him and he nearly dropped to his knees under its calculating charm. "Not after he's just asked me to take a stroll in the garden with him. He insisted I tell you where I'd be." Her hand slipped up his arm and settled in the crook of his elbow. "So you wouldn't worry. Isn't he simply the most *thoughtful* thing you ever laid eyes on?"

If she fluttered her eyelashes, he was out of there. But in the brief moment her gaze locked onto his, he saw only a mute appeal for him to play along. And, what the hell. This was better than the way she usually treated him. "I did suggest a moonlight stroll," he lied, smiling down at her before he turned back to her father, man-to-man being the logical next step in this farce. "I promise I'll bring your daughter back with roses in her cheeks," he added, thinking that the autumn air would probably give her goose bumps as well. But then, considering that the pediatric center didn't actually *have* a garden yet— it was still under construction—they wouldn't be strolling in it long enough to feel the nip.

"See that you do." Rick O'Reilly had already lost interest, his attention wandering to a waiter who was passing by with a tray of drinks. "You want something else to drink, Mother?"

Peyton had Matt away and out the front door before he quite knew he was on the move. "Thank you," she said in a rush when they hit the open air. "I'm so sorry. Really, really sorry. But there wasn't much time and I couldn't think of a better idea. And…well, I needed you as a distraction."

From hero to distraction in the space of a sentence. "That certainly takes the wind out of my sails," he said. "I thought you were having a change of heart."

"No, you didn't." Forehead creased, expression troubled, Peyton paced away from him, her emerald gown sashaying across the curve of her hips, rippling around her ankles. The evening dress was virtually backless, exposing an expanse of sleek, creamy skin to the cool October night, and he wondered if he should offer her his jacket.

But she seemed oblivious to the cold as she studied the parking lot, turned, and paced back to where he waited. "Where would a *lovely* young man with more car than sense take a gullible young girl with a propensity for trouble on Halloween night?"

"Your sister?"

"She would be the gullible young girl."

"And Covington Locke?"

"He would be the lovely young man."

"And you think they'll get into trouble?"

She arched an eyebrow. "Even if it wasn't Halloween."

"So why did your parents let her go?"

The other eyebrow rose. This didn't require much imagination, really. Parents who equated wealth and privilege with character and who wanted their daughter to be accepted. Two teenagers. A car. Miles of secluded beach. "Maybe they're in a group," he suggested, as if that would keep trouble at bay.

"I'm going after her." Determination thrummed through the words, her nod was mere confirmation. "Tell me the top ten list of teenage hideouts," she said. "Starting with the one you think Covington would be most likely to hit first. And then tell me how to get there."

"We'd be here all night and halfway into tomorrow. Rhode Island has over four hundred miles of coastline, much of it easily accessible and pretty secluded at night. And that's not even counting any number of inland places they might have gone."

"Well, isn't there a public curfew or something?"

This time his eyebrow lifted. "Weren't you a teenager once?"

She sighed. "Scarlett was my curfew. She kept me from getting into who knows what kind of trouble. I'm not doing a very good job at returning the favor.''

"Maybe it's not your job.''

"I thought you took care of your younger siblings.''

"I did. Our parents were away more than they were home.''

"And if it was your teenage sister out there, what would you do?''

"Go after her.''

She stood there, looking out into the dark as if she could will her sister back to the party inside, rubbing her arms against the chill and daring him without words to explain why she should not do what he'd just admitted he would.

But this was different. Her parents, however foolish they might be, were very much in the picture and bore the responsibility if—and in Matt's mind that was a fairly big *if*—Scarlett did choose to get into trouble. This was not Peyton's battle, although he could tell she was at war over it. "Let's go back inside,'' he suggested because he could see she was cold and because, bottom line, this was none of his business and not his problem. "You're cold.''

"You're wrong, Matt.'' And he knew she wasn't referring to the temperature.

"I can see you shivering,'' he said anyway.

Her gaze came back to him, calling his bluff. "I

have to try. My parents are who they are, but Scarlett shouldn't have to pay for their mistakes...or mine. She's only fifteen. He's twenty. I can see the danger in that equation, even if my mother chooses not to.''

''I thought he was closer to her age.''

''Well, he isn't. And I'm not convinced he's such a lovely young man, either. Now, if you were Covington, where would you go on a moonlight drive?''

Matt hated that he allowed Peyton to consistently back him into a corner no gentleman could gracefully get out of. ''I'll take you,'' he said. ''But you have to get a coat. And I can't guarantee we'll find them.''

She walked up to him, close enough for him to catch the scent of some exotic perfume, close enough for him to see a familiar fire in her eyes. ''I wasn't asking you to take me. All I'm asking for is a general direction.''

At that moment, he wanted to shake her only slightly less than he wanted to kiss her. He wasn't stupid enough to do either, so he reached for her arm, felt the chill on her and the rocket flash of heat that sliced under his skin and shot like fire up through his veins. ''You'll be lost before you get anywhere near those kids,'' he said a little more roughly than he intended. ''I said I'd take you and I will.''

"Don't be ridiculous. This is Ainsley's wedding reception. You can't go missing. And it's totally unnecessary. Scarlett is my sister. I'll find her. I never meant for you to get involved."

"Get your coat," Matt growled, and opening the door, he escorted her—a little forcefully—inside. "And please, don't make a scene. This is, after all, a happy occasion."

She looked up at him and a dual fire of anger and desire burned between them. Passion—that uninvited, unacknowledged guest—danced in the flames. "Thank you," she replied tightly, "but I don't need—"

"—my help," he finished for her. "I understand. Now, get your coat."

She stood her ground for a moment, but then she turned abruptly and walked away, offering him a long view of her bare back and the taut, seductive sway of her hips. He knew, absolutely, there was no seduction in her thoughts—if he was even still in her thoughts—and that she'd be horrified if she could read his. Hell, he felt horrified enough for both of them. And furious that he'd let himself get involved in her problems. He should be out there dancing with one or the other of his sisters…or any number of other beautiful, and agreeable, partners.

But even as he tried to convince himself he was unhappy at this unexpected turn of events, he knew it was a lie. Peyton had offered him exactly what he wanted—an opportunity to escape the happiness that surrounded and threatened to suffocate him. He adored Ainsley, was truly glad she'd married his best friend. He was happy that Miranda had found Nate. He always felt pleased to see his parents. And yet, he never trusted happiness, had never quite managed to befriend it. Too much of a good thing was still too much, and the truth was, he'd prefer a futile search in the dark with a woman he barely knew than to stay and witness the changes that were already in motion for the women he loved.

It wasn't right. Or fair. Or particularly mature. But there it was. And, as much as he hated having to admit it even to himself, Matt knew that if Peyton hadn't provided this chance to escape, he would simply have found another excuse.

"Something to drink, Mr. Danville?"

He shook his head at the waiter, then gauging Peyton's progress in retrieving her coat, he slipped to the bar and snagged a bottle of wine and a couple of glasses. However the rest of this evening turned out, he figured that somewhere in the night, he was going to need a drink.

AINSLEY LOOPED her arms around Ivan's neck and smiled at him as they danced, swaying in one place, wrapped in the light of the day's happiness. "Well,

Mrs. Donovan, you're looking especially pleased with yourself,'' he said. ''That secretive little smile wouldn't have anything to do with your big brother's mysterious disappearance, would it?''

''Now, why would I be happy that Matt walked out on my wedding reception and hasn't returned?'' But she was happy. Happy to be Ivan's wife. Happy that Matt and Peyton had left together. Happy to think her impulsive *introduction of possibilities* had taken effect so quickly. She hadn't expected that. Not at all. But it did add an extra dollop to her happiness level, which was spilling over as it was. ''He didn't even say goodbye to me.''

''I imagine he feels there'll be opportunities for goodbyes tomorrow at the family brunch.'' Ivan leaned in, pressed his cheek against her hair. ''It is my personal opinion that right now you're ecstatic because he left with Peyton O'Reilly more than an hour ago and we haven't seen either of them since. I'd say you're thinking you've successfully introduced Matt to the possibility that he has met his match in Peyton.''

She drew back to caution him. ''Shh, Ivan. Talking about it could jinx it. Just because they left together tonight doesn't mean we can call my matchmaking a success.'' She offered up a conspiratorial smile. ''Although I'm feeling *very* optimistic. I've known for *ages* that if the two of them were ever alone together long enough, they'd figure out there was a reason their discussions are so passionate.''

''I can't believe you've been playing matchmaker at our wedding, Mrs. Donovan. Couldn't you take the day off?''

She feigned an expression of grievous resignation. ''You'll simply have to get used to it, Ivan. A matchmaker's lot in life is to find opportunities wherever and whenever they present themselves. It's a full-time job, especially for an apprentice matchmaker like me.''

''You *are* taking two weeks off for our honeymoon, though, right? No matchmaking will be taking place in Italy.''

She lifted her shoulders in a dainty shrug. ''I can't promise, Ivan, but I expect I'll be too busy to think much about my career, especially with all the sightseeing and so on we'll be doing.''

''I certainly intend to keep you busy with the *so on* part.''

She giggled, thrilled at the prospect of having his undivided attention for two entire weeks. ''I bought a tour book called *See Italy in a Weekend*. But as creative as you and I are, I imagine we could squeeze all the highlights into half a day, don't you?''

''I do,'' he said, and whirled her around the dance

floor, the bride and groom celebrating this one moment…and all the moments still to come.

"THEY'RE NOT HERE, either." Matt swung the car around in a slow U-turn, allowing the beam from the headlights to sweep across the deserted park. Not another car in sight. No sign of two young people looking for trouble. No sign of anyone else at all. "And, frankly, I don't know where else to look."

She glanced at him in the semidarkness of the car's interior, noting that his classically handsome features revealed no hint of the impatience she knew he must be feeling. But he'd insisted on driving, insisted on accompanying her, despite *her* insistence that it wasn't necessary. And she wasn't ready to give up. "Oh, come on, Matt. You must remember your misspent youth and the places you took girls when you were Covington's age."

"That was a long time ago, and my youth was never as misspent as you might think."

She sighed. "Neither was mine. But Scarlett seems determined to more than make up for my prudence."

"I, somehow, have trouble associating you with prudence at any stage of your life."

"I've learned to speak my mind, if that's what you mean. But just because I won't allow you—or anyone else—to trample on my opinions, doesn't mean I go out of my way to take foolish chances.''

''Oh,'' he said, aggravating her with the arrogance of the single syllable.

''*Oh*, is right. We are talking about two different things and I'd be happy to argue my point, but I think it's much more important to find my sister. Where did you take girls when you wanted to be alone with them?''

His jaw tightened and he looked out the window for a moment, uncomfortable with the question or the answer. She neither knew nor cared which. ''It is possible, Peyton, that they're at a club somewhere listening to a band and having a couple of beers.''

''She's fifteen, Matt. Covington is twenty and should know better than to take her anywhere, especially where alcohol is served.''

He put the car in gear. ''We'll drive over to the Cape. When I wanted to be alone for any reason, I went to our beach house. The Lockes have one that's two doors down from ours. I probably should have thought of checking there first.''

She was grateful—more, really, than she wanted to admit—that he was willing to help her. She was appreciative of his concern for her sister. But mostly, she was thankful that the night concealed the wistful hunger inside her, kept him from seeing in her eyes that she wished he were taking her to his beach house, that instead of searching futilely for her foolish sister, she could have just one chance to be foolish herself.

The thought itself was foolish. She knew that. But as they sped into the night, shut inside the sports car, she couldn't help wondering what might happen if she could forget only for a little while about being responsible, about what was the right thing to do, and give in to the attraction that burned like a fever beneath her skin.

She glanced at Matt as the car approached the bridge that would take them over to Cape Cod. And she wondered if they didn't find Scarlett at the Lockes' Cape Cod house, would Matt, perhaps, suggest a stop at his beach house?

And what might happen if he did?

Chapter Two

Matt took off his topcoat, gave it a shake to discourage the snowflakes from settling into the wool and hung it on the coat tree in the outer office. "T.J.," he said. "What's wrong with the music?"

His student assistant and gofer during the morning hours looked up from a huge, open textbook with a dazed, historical-facts frown and listened to the piped-in sound for a few seconds. "I think it's 'Jingle Bells'," he said.

"My point exactly." Matt cocked his head, inviting T.J. to pay closer attention. "*That* is the same song I heard at least two dozen times yesterday and the day before and the day before that *and* the day before that. I'm telling you, there's a virus or something in the airwaves."

"Well, it's Christmas," practical T.J. pointed out as he presented Matt with a sheaf of message slips with one hand while holding his place in the textbook with the other. "If x equals the number of holiday tunes and y is the number of days between Thanksgiving and Christmas, then depending on how you want to calculate it, z is the number of times you're going to hear 'Jingle Bells'."

"Z is about two thousand times too many."

"Do you want me to cancel the Muzak service?"

"An excellent idea, T.J. Except that if x equals the number of people in this building who like 'Jingle Bells' and y equals the number who don't, then z is the number of screams I'm going to hear if I cancel the holiday music."

T.J. frowned, considering possible solutions to that equation. "I guess you can borrow my earmuffs." He reached under the desk for his backpack and offered up a sorry-looking pair of muffs.

"Thanks, but I think I'll just check into canceling Christmas altogether."

"Oh, okay. Well, they're here if you want them." The earmuffs disappeared under the desk again and T.J. went back to his history lesson.

Matt entered his private office and closed the door behind him, thinking "Jingle Bells" might stay on the other side. But the music drifted in, bright as tinsel, a melody on amphetamines, overorchestrated into a galloping, get-with-the-spirit-or-else intrusion. He was not in the mood to get in the spirit, not in the mood for the looming holidays, not in the mood to do much except stare out the window at the sputtering snowfall.

Instead, he took his seat behind the ornately carved wooden desk that had passed from one industrious Jonathan to the next for a couple of centuries. The leather chair sighed and creaked as it settled beneath his weight into a supple, familiar comfort. Heat shushed through the air register. ''Jingle Bells'' switched over to ''Jingle Bell Rock'' and somewhere out on the water a ship's horn brayed. Matt tossed the phone slips aside and turned on his computer. A list of messages popped up on the screen almost instantly. A dozen Merry Christmas greetings. A dozen more generic Happy Holidays, one Happy Hanukkah, and two credit card offers. Scattered among the greetings were five interoffice messages—two marked with a flashing *red* urgent!—a forwarded joke, two unsolicited *Thoughts for the Day,* a reminder that he was expected at the Freemans' annual Hijacked Holiday dinner party tomorrow evening and an invitation to yet another holiday get-together between Christmas and New Year's Eve at the Stamfords'.

''Bah humbug,'' he muttered and turned off the computer.

He picked up the phone messages again, sorting through them with misdirected irritation. Jessica. Jessica. Jessica. Ainsley. Miranda. And Ainsley, again. He didn't want to talk to Jessica because he knew that, sooner or later, she'd turn the conversation toward some new or imagined grievance Peyton O'Reilly had caused. He didn't want to talk to Ainsley because her conversation always included something especially funny or endearing her friend, Peyton O'Reilly, had done or said. Ainsley wasn't giving up on her plan of making a match for him and Peyton, despite his attempts to discourage her. Ainsley blithely disregarded his resistance and continued to find ways to bring Peyton's name into almost any conversation. Miranda didn't talk about Peyton O'Reilly, but then he didn't really want to hear about Nate's two sets of twins, either. If Andy had called and left a message, Matt would have returned the call in a heartbeat. But wise Andrew had scheduled a trip to Utah and, at this very moment, was likely hiking up or skiing down some blessedly quiet mountain trail. Matt figured his little brother hadn't heard "Jingle Bells" in at least twenty-four hours. Maybe longer.

"Merry Christmas, Matt!!" Ainsley's cheery greeting came through ahead of her as she opened the door and walked in. Her cheeks were flushed and rosy from the cold, her blond curls peeked out from under a Christmas-green stocking hat, her upper body was bundled in a fleecy Christmas-green coat, her pants were black, her boots red, and there was a sparkly gold scarf looped like a garland around her neck.

"Are you dressed like a Christmas tree on purpose?" he asked, getting up to accept a hug even as he turned his smile from her to her companion.

Miranda looked equally healthy, happy and fetching, although she wasn't dressed remotely like a holiday icon. All in ivory, hair sleek and secured beneath a hat as stylish as practical, her smile was pure confidence, with more than a hint of excitement. "Merry Christmas, Matt!" She switched on the overhead, flooding the dimly lit office with wattage. "It is okay to turn on a light when you're actually in your office, you know. It's only when you leave for the day that you need to make sure it's off."

"I'm experimenting," he said.

"With eyestrain?"

"With the theory that this constant bombardment of Christmas music will be less irritating in the dark."

"Well, bah humbug to you, too." Ainsley thumped him playfully on the arm. "But never fear. We are here to improve your attitude, lighten your spirits and take you out for lunch. Our treat. And we won't take no for an answer, so don't even bother with an excuse."

"I just got here," he said. "I had a breakfast meeting that lasted all morning and I have about ten

minutes before I have to meet Jessica for lunch.''
He paused, then added. ''A *working* lunch.''

Ainsley and Miranda exchanged a look—one of
those sister moments they seemed to be sharing on
a regular basis these days. Then, having come to
some mutual and mysterious understanding, Miranda walked around the desk and picked up the
phone. ''T.J.,'' she said a moment later, ''call Ms.
Martin-Kingsley and tell her Matt has an unexpected
family situation and won't be able to keep their lun-
cheon appointment.'' She listened for a moment,
then laughed. ''That's right. She'll have to work
without him. Thanks, T.J.''

She hung up, smiled at Matt. ''Fancy that. You're
free for lunch.''

''Is this an unexpected family situation?''

Ainsley slipped her arm through his, beamed up
at him. ''You weren't expecting us, we're family
and we're hungry.''

Miranda gestured *voila!* ''An unexpected family
situation. Besides, Matthew, you do not want to
spend any more time with Jessica than you absolutely have to. It gives me a headache just to think
about her.''

It often gave him one, too, but then, lately, think-
ing about women in general had the same effect.
''Great,'' he said. ''You two are taking me to lunch.
Where are we going?''

"The Red Parrot?" Miranda suggested with a questioning glance to Ainsley.

"Suits me." Ainsley gave Matt's arm a gentle tug. "Is Peyton here today?" she asked as they moved toward the door. "We should ask her to join us."

"Oh, that's a good idea." Miranda's comment was so quick, so close on the heels of Ainsley's impromptu thought, that Matt would have had to be thicker than a slab of bacon not to realize this whole lunch scheme was a setup, put together and practiced ahead of time by his sisters for his ultimate good.

And that, in a nutshell, was the problem with women.

They believed a man could be improved, should be improved, and they were always eager to introduce him to a woman they thought was up to the task. He loved his sisters, liked and respected the men they'd chosen, believed each of them was better for having found the other. But that kind of relationship wasn't for him. And it sure as hell wasn't for him with Peyton. He'd come too close for comfort to thinking it might be possible not so very long ago and gotten burned for his effort. No, thank you.

"I've no idea where Ms. O'Reilly might be," he said with a smile meant to convey benign indifference. "But I can guarantee she won't want to have lunch with me."

"And what makes you so sure of that?" Ainsley's eyes sparkled with secrets and innuendo.

"Oh, maybe the fact that our every conversation seems to turn into an argument." Which wasn't true, although it wasn't entirely a lie, either. "Or maybe because she's been avoiding me as much as possible for the past two months." Which was true. He'd been avoiding her, too, but that was irrelevant. "Or maybe it's because I'm on to this little matchmaking plan of yours and, for the record, I'm not interested. Never have been." Which was a lie. "And never will be." *Again.* Which was the truth.

The sparkle in Baby's eyes merely brightened. "Wow, you've obviously given that a lot of thought." Her gaze went to Miranda and some glimmer of understanding passed between the two women again. "Guess we won't invite Peyton to lunch today."

"Guess not," Miranda said. "Guess we'll just have to keep him all to ourselves."

"Guess so." Ainsley gave his arm a squeeze. "But, don't worry, we'll share you when the right woman comes along."

"I'm not worried," he replied. "Because the right woman isn't going to come along for a very, very, *very* long time. If ever."

Ainsley's laugh conveyed more clearly than words just how much confidence she'd gained as a matchmaker during the past year. The smile she exchanged with Miranda told him she clearly had her romantic wand aimed at him. And clearly, Miranda also thought that he was a prime candidate for a makeover.

Protest was futile. But forewarned is forearmed, and he happened to know a few facts his sisters didn't know. Weren't ever going to know. So, let them plot to their hearts' content. It would come to nothing, anyway. He and Peyton had agreed. And as far as he was concerned, that was the end of it.

PEYTON PUSHED her plate away, hoping no one would notice that she'd managed to massacre the cheeseburger, mangle and scatter the fries without eating a single bite. But, of course, no one would notice. The waiter was just trying to survive the lunch crowd. He didn't care what food she left on her plate as long as he received his tip. Her lunch companion was even less interested than the waiter. Scarlett, at fifteen, was consumed with her own orbit, and barely aware that anyone else had a life apart from how it intersected with her own.

"You are *not* going to *believe* what she said after *that*." Scarlett talked with a French fry, waving it like a baton before dipping it into first ketchup, then mayonnaise, then biting off the end. "'It's the *silver* Donna Karan or the *blue* Vera Wang, Scarlett.'" She imitated their mother's voice down to the imprecise slur of her Louisiana drawl. "'You cannot have *both.* You do not need *both.* You may choose *one,* not *both.*'" Scarlett double-dipped and bit again, chewing the fried potato as she pondered their mother's complete ignorance. "I mean, *puh-lease!* As if I'd be caught *dead* in Karan or Wang! How can she *think* for one second I'd *want* to wear *anything* by a designer *she* likes?"

It was taken for granted, of course, that Peyton would agree. She was Scarlett's main sounding board. At least when it came to discussing their mother. "How *could* Mother think you'd be interested in a dress by either of those very famous, very talented designers?" Peyton said. "Honestly, sometimes I think she does it just to torture you."

Scarlett raised her perfect eyebrows and leveled a ketchup-smeared French fry for emphasis. "Don't side with Mom, Peyton. Just because they couldn't afford to buy you nice clothes when you were my age is no reason I should have to wear something I hate." The ketchup end of the fry went into the lump of mayo and from there into Scarlett's mouth. "Besides, this is a *very* special date for me. It's *important,* and the dress *has* to be perfect."

Here was the subject Peyton wanted to talk about

and she chose her words carefully. "To impress Covington?"

"No, to impress Covington's mother and father." Her green eyes nailed Peyton's best intentions. "I want Mr. and Mrs. Locke to see that even Louisiana swamp rats look pretty good in expensive clothes." Scarlett was quick and had that uncanny teenagers' knack of putting others on the defensive. "You have such a chip on your shoulder, Peyton. I don't know why you bothered to move up here with us if all you're going to do is find fault with every single boy I like just because he can trace his ancestry back to Plymouth Rock!"

"That's not fair, Scarlett. I simply think Covington is too old for you."

"He's twenty. Five freaking years. Big deal."

"At fifteen, five years is a big deal. He's halfway through college. You're still in high school. That difference in experience is a very big deal."

"Mom doesn't think so." She played her ace casually, picked up another fry, changed the routine by skipping the ketchup, dipping only in the mayonnaise. "She likes Covington and thinks he's perfect for me. *She* knows I'm very mature for my age."

"So, as long as her opinions coincide with yours, then she really knows what she's talking about."

"If she thought Covington was too old for me,

you'd be saying how smart she is. So why is it such a freaking sin that this time she happens to agree with me?''

Peyton had hoped to have a reasonable discussion. She'd thought she could say what neither of her parents would. She'd believed, foolishly it seemed, that Scarlett would listen to her. "Mother is easily…dazzled. She wants you to fit in so badly that she's not giving you appropriate guidance. You're fifteen. He's twenty. *Twenty,* Scarlett. You should be dating boys your own age and, quite frankly, Covington should not be interested in dating someone so much younger than he is.''

Scarlett's eyes flashed fury at the criticism. "That just shows how little you know, Peyton. For your information, Covington tells me I'm a lot more mature than the college girls he knows.''

"You're underage, Scarlett, no matter how mature you may be. You have no business going to fraternity parties and he has no business inviting you. It's not fair for him or anyone else to put you in situations you shouldn't be in, situations that require choices you're not ready to make.''

"How would you know? You never went to a fraternity party. You hardly ever even went out on a date. You went to class and came home. That's it. You didn't even live on campus.''

"I had to stay with you," she retorted in self-defense. "Mom and Dad were working, and I didn't live on campus so I could stay with you."

"I never asked you to do that. I'll bet Mom and Dad didn't ask you to, either. You did it because you were too scared to go away to school. Or you did it because you liked feeling needed. I don't know why you did it, and I don't care." She tossed the French fry onto her plate, wadded up her napkin, glared across the table. "I'm not going to make the mistakes you did, Peyton. By the time *I'm* twenty-seven, I'll have had a million times more fun than you ever thought about having. And I'll *still* turn out to be a whole heck of a lot smarter than you are now."

That stung. Because it was true. Scarlett would have to be incredibly stupid, even at fifteen, to wind up in the situation Peyton now found herself in. *Found herself.* As if she hadn't had a thing to do with getting there. As if she hadn't, against every atom of good judgment, every molecule of good sense, willingly and willfully, made a really, really bad choice. And now she *found herself* without options.

Or at least without any options she wanted.

"Thanks for lunch." The chair scraped across the floor as Scarlett pushed up from the table. "And thanks for caring, but the truth is I already have a mother. I don't need another one." She spun on her heel and flounced across the restaurant to the door, her slip of a purse bouncing against her slim little hip, her long dark hair swishing across her shoulders, her flippy strut and flippant attitude signaling her indignation.

And she was right.

Totally wrong in what she wanted, and was being allowed, to do. But absolutely right in thinking a sister had no authority to correct a parent's mistake.

Peyton folded her own napkin, laid it beside her plate and waited for the bill to be delivered. She didn't know why she'd ever thought talking to Scarlett about this was a good idea. She hadn't been able to get her mother to see sense. Or her dad. So what had made her think she could persuade Scarlett? What had made her believe it was her duty to try?

She'd given up any claim to being a role model the night of Ainsley Danville's wedding, the night she and Matt had gone looking for Scarlett.

They hadn't found Scarlett or Covington, though it hadn't been for lack of searching.

Oh, no, the lack had come later.

But she wasn't going back over that night again. Not the worst of it. Not the best of it. If she could turn back the clock and change it all, from start to finish, she would. She'd stay at the party, stay out of Matt's car, stay away from any possibility of finding herself in this…this untenable situation. But that door was closed. She had slammed it shut behind her, and now she had to follow the detour she had impetuously, and so unwisely, chosen.

The waiter brought the check; she gave him money and he returned with change, and she left it all on the table. She drank her ice water and let him refill the glass twice before, finally, pulling on her gloves, her coat, her scarf and heading out into the cold December air.

She hadn't planned to see Matt Danville this afternoon, but the day was already ruined, her stomach already knotted with tension. And it wasn't as if there would ever be a good time to face him and say the words that needed to be said. Nothing about this was going to be easy, no matter how much longer she put it off. So she might as well do it now, while the sky matched her mood and the air was cold enough to numb a heavy heart.

THE SNOWFLAKES of the morning had long since turned into a gray drizzle, but Matt swiveled his chair and stared out the rain-slicked window at the dreary afternoon. As if he had nothing to do. As if daydreaming was his main occupation. He had plenty of work awaiting him. Important work. Necessary work. Work that meant a world of difference to a child halfway around the world. A child he would never meet.

The wind chased a raindrop across the window-pane, leaving a wavy trail across the glass. A second drop splattered and raced to oblivion in three tiny rivulets. He wished that he could love this work, wished that it brought him the soul-deep satisfaction it should. But he seemed to lack something, some fundamental *Jonathan* element missing that left him dissatisfied and restless in his life. Which, right now, happened to be the reason he sat staring out the window at a dismal view instead of turning his mind to work that was worthy and rewarding and, by birth-right, his to do.

He heard a soft footfall and the rustle of move-ment in the outer office, caught the scent of an elu-sive perfume and felt a twinge of regret that his solitude was about to be interrupted. T.J. attended classes in the afternoons. Jenny, the afternoon stu-dent assistant, was off sick with a cold. The Foun-dation offices seemed uncommonly quiet on this rainy day and, when he heard the soft tap on his opened door, he fully expected to turn and see Jes-sica standing in the doorway, one excuse or another tucked under her arm.

But when he swiveled around, it was Peyton who stood there, her coat unbuttoned and splotched from the rain, a plaid Christmas scarf hanging listlessly from her collar, her dark hair curling slightly with the damp. She appeared pale, hesitant, as if she'd rather be anywhere else as she drew a glove off first one hand, then the other. The sudden unwitting thrill of seeing her so unexpectedly faded as her eyes met his and her expression turned cool and distant. He missed the fire of her arguments, the zeal she'd thrown at him for no better reason than that she enjoyed their debates. But since the night at the beach house, she and her passionate opinions had avoided him. It made him think she'd expended all the passion she had to offer him that night and nothing but indifference remained. The fact that she was here, now, in his office, looking as if a breath of controversy would blow her away, annoyed him, and that annoyance was both illogical and inconvenient. But he rose, like a gentleman, and offered her a polite smile. "Peyton," he said, her name forming a stern, stiff greeting.

"Matt," she returned evenly, waiting in the doorway of his office for an invitation to come in, an invitation she seemed to know he didn't want to extend. "Do you have a minute?"

"Actually, no." He glanced at his watch, reluctant to be in her presence any longer than absolutely necessary, regretting the discomfort he seemed to cause her, too. "I'm due in Providence in an hour and should already be on my way. Jessica's in her office, though. Why don't you talk to her about whatever's on your mind and she can fill me in later.''

''I could do that, but I don't really think you want her to be the first to know that we're pregnant.''

The word slammed into him. A sucker punch. ''Come in,'' he said. ''Close the door.''

She stepped into the room, closed the door behind her, waited, perhaps for further instructions.

He had none for her, couldn't have formed a cohesive thought if she'd put a gun to his head. *Pregnant.* The word pounded in his head, clawed at his composure, pummeled his gut with fear. Like a reel of film spinning too fast, his memory clicked off the events leading to this moment. The wedding reception. Her distress. Searching for her sister. The moon. The ocean. The decision to try the Lockes' beach house on Cape Cod. His suggestion to stop at the Danville beach house for a break and a glass of wine. Her unexpected kiss. His unexpected response. One thing leading to another. The morning after. Her saying it was a mistake. His relief that she thought so, too. Their agreement to behave as if nothing had happened, to forget that anything had. And now…

He gestured to a chair and, without waiting for her to take a seat, he sank, weak-kneed, into his own. ''Would you…say that one more time?''

"Pregnant," she repeated. "You and I. We're pregnant."

He hated the way she said it. *He* wasn't pregnant. Couldn't *be* pregnant. How could this not be some ridiculous mistake? "Peyton, I don't see how that could be poss—"

"Do *not* say it's impossible," she cut him off quickly, forcefully. "You know exactly how, and when, it happened."

"But—"

"Yes," she interrupted again. "I'm sure. *Yes,* I'm positive you're the father. And *yes,* I'm going to have the baby."

He clasped his hands together, pressed them hard against the desk to hide their trembling. A thousand denials jockeyed for position in his thoughts. This couldn't be true, couldn't be happening. Not to him. Not with her. She sat facing him, looking calm if not serene, steady if not comfortable, the proof of her statements written in the shadows beneath her eyes, the terrible tension in her stillness. The weight of a dark acceptance settled into his shoulders, forced his head down until his forehead rested on his clenched fists. One night. One careless, stupid night out of a lifetime of careful, considerate choices. One foolish bet with fate in thirty-four years of dutiful caution. One night of flirting with an attraction he'd known should not be acknowledged much less encouraged. He was responsible and yet he blamed Peyton, wanted to stamp her with fault, label her a seductress and sidestep the consequences. To hell with the truth.

One night…and he was caught like the rat he'd always somehow suspected he was.

"I know this is a shock," she said…and there might even have been the taint of compassion in her voice. "I'm sorry."

He raised his head, gave her a stony stare. "Sorry for the shock? Or sorry we were so stupid?"

"Does it matter?"

No, but he needed something to justify his rising anger. "How long have you known?"

"Six weeks. I've been certain for four."

"And you're just now telling me?"

She didn't even blink. "I had to make some decisions."

"Decisions I could have no part in making, even though they'll affect my life as much as yours?"

Her lips parted. He could all but see the excuses ready to spill out of her. But then she stopped, toyed with the fringe of her scarf. "Look, maybe I should go, give you some time to come to grips with this. We can talk later. After the holiday, maybe."

"We'll talk now." The anger washed through him in a self-righteous, contemptuous wave. He hated this, hated her, hated himself for being in a situation he was too old and too responsible to be in. And yet, here he was, as good an example of poor judgment and bad behavior as any hormonal teenager. But so much worse…because he knew better and had not a single excuse. "Why don't you tell me what you've decided, Peyton."

"You won't like it."

"I think that's pretty much a given."

She shifted slightly in the chair, tugged the fringe of her scarf through her fingers until her knuckles showed white with the strain. But when she met his gaze, when she spoke, there wasn't even a hint of uncertainty. "We can do this one of two ways, Matt. We can agree that this conversation never took place. I'll walk out that door, move away and out of your life. This child will be mine. You'll bear no responsibility and have no claim. Not now, or at any time in the future. I'll say I wanted a baby and went to a fertility clinic and that I have no idea who the father is." Her eyes blazed with the conviction that was rock solid in her voice, scaring him a little with her intensity. "I'll go to my grave with the secret, Matt, but you must agree to do the same."

"I can't do that." He hadn't known that was the truth until he heard the words, felt the *rightness* of them resonate inside him. "I won't do that. What's the other option?"

"We do this together, starting now and with an equal commitment to the welfare of our child."

"That, at least, sounds reasonable."

"There's a catch."

"A catch to giving this child two parents instead of one?"

She swallowed, the only sign of hesitancy she'd shown so far. "The devil is always in the details, Matt. If you're going to acknowledge this baby, then you're going to acknowledge me as well."

"Meaning?"

"Meaning that I expect you to marry me."

"You can't be serious." But he could see she was. "No," he said. "That is not going to happen. Even I know better than to complicate one mistake by making an even bigger one."

Her color—what little she'd had—seeped out of her cheeks and she looked newly fragile. "I don't want my child to grow up thinking he was a mistake."

"It's a little late to think of that, Peyton."

Anger flared in her eyes, tightened the corners of her lips. "Don't patronize me. This is our mistake, Matt. Yours and mine. Our child should not have to pay for it."

"And how is having parents who are in a disastrous marriage going to keep that from happening?"

"Look, I have no illusions that we're going to

live happily ever after. I'm not asking for that. All I want is a beginning. A foundation. For the baby. For us, as his parents.''

''A foundation?''

''The months of the pregnancy, plus one year. After that, we can divorce and lead separate lives.''

''Holy hell, Peyton.'' He ran a hand through his hair, unable to believe he was having this conversation. ''You want me to marry you so we can divorce as soon as the baby turns a year old? What kind of foundation is that?''

''A good one. One that removes the stigma of illegitimacy. One that provides the opportunity for us to get to know each other. We're virtual strangers now, but don't kid yourself, Matt, we are going to share something very important for the rest of our lives. A whole new person. A whole other life. All the people who will interact with that new life, all the events that will impact it, will be part of our lives, too. We're going to be spending time together and making decisions together whether we want to or not. How can we expect to raise a child who has any true sense of his place in the world if we can't figure out how to have a discussion that doesn't end in an argument? We can't go back and undo what we've done. We can't make a perfect environment from our recklessness. But we can learn how to be friends, how to parent together, how to parent apart, how to share the single most important job either of us will ever do.''

She was utterly convinced…and almost irresistibly convincing. Matt knew there were layers of misjudgment in her argument, knew she hadn't thought this out to its logical conclusion, but he wasn't thinking too clearly, either. His heart had gotten tangled up in a few random words. *A whole new person. The single most important job.* They were going to have a baby.

He looked at her, at the spark of conviction in her shadowed eyes, at the pale resolve that anchored the corner of her lips, and he was stricken with the inexplicable yearning to gather her into his arms and hold her there, their hearts beating out a single rhythm of reassurance to the child whose heartbeat was still, as yet, undetectable between them.

"I don't know, Peyton," he said. "Marriage should mean something, from the start."

"So should making a baby."

He had no comeback for that, only a thick, achy guilt that lodged deep in his chest.

She twisted the fringe again, gave a deep, long sigh. "I know this isn't a great solution, Matt. I know it complicates an already complicated situation. I know it isn't what you want and it certainly isn't what I had in mind for my life. But we made a choice two months ago that changed all that. If we were different people, in different circumstances, I'd be the first to admit that marriage probably isn't the best option for us. But we're who we are, our families are what they are, and in many ways we both live in glass houses. Your position here at the Danville Foundation is all about image and my family is vastly concerned about the minutiae of fitting in. If I thought none of that would affect our baby, I'd be out the door and heading back home to Louisiana in a New York minute. If I could believe that being born outside the sanction of marriage would have no more impact on this child than a…a birthmark, this conversation could move on to who'll buy the bassinet and who'll get the diapers.'' She released her hold on the fringe and scooted forward in the chair, preparing to stand. ''I don't expect you to agree with me, Matt.'' A slight smile lightened her expression, made the whole office seem somehow a bit brighter. ''Well, I guess I do expect you to agree, but I've had six weeks to wrestle with the ins and outs of this. I can understand that it may take you a little longer than fifteen minutes to reach the same conclusion.''

Now, *that* was the Peyton he knew. ''That's what I like about you, Peyton,'' he said with the easy familiarity he'd thought they had lost for good. ''You may be wrong, but you're never uncertain.''

Her smile came close to full power. ''For future

reference, Matt, you should probably keep in mind that I'm not often wrong, either.''

Strangely enough, he found himself smiling, too, as she stood and reached into her pocket for the gloves she'd tucked inside. Rising, he wondered if it was still raining, if he should offer her his umbrella or walk her out to her car. She seemed a little fragile…or was that merely his shifting perception? He knew pregnancy didn't necessarily equate to physical weakness, and yet he was suddenly swarmed with protective instincts as he came around the desk and accompanied her to the door. Should he take her elbow, offer support? Maybe he should insist on taking her home.

She turned in the doorway, catching him within her comfort zone, sparking the attraction that wasn't supposed to still be there. She took a step back. So did he. ''Let me know when you're ready to talk again,'' she said. ''I'm going to Baton Rouge to visit a friend the day after Christmas, but I'll be back before New Year's.''

''Should you be flying?'' It was out of his mouth before he could stop it and he felt ridiculous for asking.

She didn't answer, just took her time, tucking the scarf inside the coat, drawing on the knitted gloves. ''I'll wait for your call, Matt.''

He opened the door, kept his distance as she

walked out. She paused, looked back at him over her shoulder, offered another small smile. "I'm sorry it happened this way, but I'm hopeful we can figure out how to be friends."

She was gone before he could reply and long before he admitted to himself that he hoped so, too.

Chapter Three

Christmas arrived with Ainsley's giggle.

Until she came through the front doors of Danfair, bundled in her Christmas tree ensemble, toting an armload of presents and a bubbly, excited air of anticipation, Matt had written off the holiday as a lost cause. He'd spent days in a fog of jumbled thoughts and fluctuating emotions, one minute angry as hell and raging with denial and self-recrimination, the next minute coldly self-loathing and detached, planning the most rational way to handle the situation…and Peyton.

Marriage.

As if *that* was a sane idea.

"Matt! Merry Christmas!" Ainsley's eyes shone bright with excitement as she came up on tiptoe and leaned over the stack of gaily wrapped packages in her arms to kiss him on the cheek. "You're going to be so happy when you see what I got you this year! Ivan got you a present, too, but it's not nearly as great as my gift.'' She thrust the packages into his arms and began stripping off her gloves. ''Would you help Ivan get the rest of the stuff out of the car? Where's Andrew? What did he break this time? He was hotdogging, wasn't he? Is he *ever* going to grow up?''

She whisked off to the North Salon to find her twin, trailing coat, muffler and questions behind her, leaving Matt to feel that, at last, Christmas had come to Danfair.

The house had been unnaturally quiet in the two months since Ainsley's wedding. Miranda was seldom home, spending most of her time—and a lot of her organizational energies—with Nate and his kids, either at his coffeehouse, A New Brew, or at his house, which was only a few blocks away, but might as well have been located clear across the country. For all intents and purposes, Miranda had already left home. Andrew, too, came and went, camera bag in hand, following his own agenda, spending a good deal of time at his studio and using Danfair more as a port of call than a home base. He'd returned yesterday from his ski trip, sporting a bright blue cast on his right ankle, a couple of nasty bruises and a complementary black eye.

As Andrew incidents went, it wasn't that bad. He'd suffered much worse, on a regular basis, as a gawky kid, and could easily claim more scrapes, stitches, bruises, black eyes, chipped teeth and broken limbs than the rest of the Danvilles combined. Including cousins. Today, the sisters would give him due sympathy and tease him unmercifully for months to come, but he'd accept their sympathy, shrug off their teasing and be off on another quest the minute one called to him. In a day or two—certainly no less than a week—he'd be gone again, tracking the perfect photo op, searching for the one picture worth a thousand words. A broken ankle wouldn't stop him. Nothing so simple ever had. Or could. Andrew had always considered life an adventure, a trek into uncharted territory, and the more obstacles he had to overcome, the more he enjoyed the journey.

Matt had always envied him his daring, along with the freedom he had to come and go as he pleased. He admired the talent Andy accepted as if it were no big deal and the privilege of being able to take his job with him wherever he wanted, or happened, to go. Matt could only imagine that kind of autonomy. His own roots were planted straight and deep in the soil of Danfair, in the history of his family. His career was anchored fast in the traditions and moral commitments of his parents…and their parents before them. His life journey had been charted out for him from birth. He was the firstborn son of the firstborn son, the Jonathan of his generation. The weight of expectation had settled on his shoulders early and he couldn't recall a time when he hadn't behaved in a manner that suited his position…a dutiful, responsible, diligent and gentlemanly manner.

So how had he managed, in one rash, reckless night, to throw all that aside and carelessly wreck his life's plan?

And what would his family think of him once they knew?

Matt could imagine them all supportive, but quietly, silently disappointed in his choices, in him. How could he expect any other reaction? They couldn't be any more disappointed in him than he was in himself. That night with Peyton had been so out of character for him, he could still hardly believe it had happened…that he'd *allowed* it to happen. He had enjoyed the hell out of it, too, which somehow made the whole thing worse. In hindsight, he could view the event as a repercussion of the changes happening all around him, a reaction to Ainsley's wedding, Miranda's engagement and his own dissatisfaction with his work. After the fact, he could rationalize his foolhardy actions as an attempt to escape a life that sometimes felt too much like someone else's. But in reality, that night at the beach house, the driving force behind his loss of control, the annihilation of his sanity, had been the sheer power of the sexual tension he and Peyton had been skirting for months. He'd been unprepared for that, blindsided by the passion that had virtually exploded between the two of them once they were alone in the forgiving dark.

"Hey, Santa Claus!" Ivan called from the doorway, struggling to keep a grip on the mountain of gifts he was trying to carry. "Can you give me a hand here?"

With a jerk, Matt came out of his reverie and hurried over to help, carting gaily wrapped packages from outside to inside, from one room to another. Gradually, lulled into reminiscences of Christmas Past by the blithe chattering of his sisters, he relaxed and let his siblings' happiness surround him with warmth. It was, after all, Christmas, and despite his situation, he had much to be grateful for.

Even without Charles and Linney, who had chosen not to come back so soon after their October visit, the house suddenly brimmed with holiday spirit and familial accord. By the time Nate arrived, with two bursting-with-excitement six-year-olds, two trying-not-to-show-their-excitement thirteen-year-olds and an abundant supply of Christmas presents, which also had to be unloaded and brought inside, Matt was feeling almost normal again.

The gift exchange flew by in a flurry of ripped

paper, discarded bows, thrilled exclamations and stacks of treasures. The morning passed with lots of laughter and the simple pleasures of a loving family gathering. By early afternoon, other guests had arrived—Nate's mother, his brother, Nick, Ivan's parents from Texas, a couple of Andrew's friends, half a dozen foreign students who worked, in one way or another, for the Foundation—and before Matt knew it, dinner was on the table, enjoyed by all, and over. The guests stayed for a while, then trickled away to other gatherings or home. Ainsley and Ivan left with his parents, Miranda left with Nate and the kids, Andrew hobbled off with his friends, and eventually Matt was left behind and alone to contemplate the Ghost of Christmas Future.

Next year, there would be a baby. His baby. The first new Danville of the next generation. A son. Or a daughter. Peyton had referred to the baby as a boy, but she couldn't know. Not this early. Matt hoped she was wrong, that the baby would be a girl. Then there'd be no question of naming her Jonathan. She could have any name at all, a family name, a whimsical name, a name that simply suited her. If the baby was a girl, her future wouldn't be laid out like a blueprint before her. She wouldn't be tied to the Foundation and it wouldn't be her responsibility to see that the Danville philosophy carried on into the next generation. If the baby was a boy, all those expectations would be his at birth. Which was why Matt had planned never to have children.

Yet he was having a child.

Next Christmas, his son or daughter would be four or five months old. If he married Peyton, they'd be more than halfway through the obligatory pregnancy plus one year commitment she'd requested. It seemed crazy to think of it that way and yet, over the course of the past week, he could see how she'd reached the conclusion that marriage offered a reasonable—and possibly the best—solution to their particular and complex situation. He didn't want to believe it, but he hadn't come up with another option that would provide the same benefits for their child. Or for the two of them. The truth was, they did live in a world of glass houses, where heritage and tradition meant more than perhaps it should, where appearance often trumped truth, and where a marriage of convenience, so long as it was kept quietly dignified, was considered an aristocratic bargain, *noblesse oblige.*

A year and seven months. Was that enough time to form a family, however fractured its beginning and its end? Would that be enough time for two strangers to become friends? Or would it make them enemies, instead? Could nineteen months of a lie really give their son or daughter a better foundation for life?

Matt thought the odds were against them, but he could see that the alternative was also a huge gamble. And whichever route he chose, he was choosing a future for his child. He didn't know if Peyton was right, if marriage was the best course. He did know he intended to be a major participant in his child's life. He knew he and Peyton had to put aside their own agendas and take responsibility for the life they'd created. He accepted that it was now their obligation to make whatever sacrifices were necessary to ensure this child had the best chance at the best life they could provide.

Next Christmas, there would be gifts under the tree for their baby from family and friends. Maybe she was right and the best gift they could offer as parents was a unified front and a family that had, at the least, started out together. It wasn't a great solution, probably not even a particularly rational one but, after much consideration, it seemed to Matt the most honorable of the alternatives before him. It was, after all, his duty to make sure that the first Danville in the next generation was born under the protective auspices of marriage, wasn't it? And, if they were careful, diligent and responsible, then only he and Peyton would ever have to know the magnitude of the lie they'd be living. This was wrong. He felt it in his gut. And yet, how could he not take the chance that in the long run, this lie would provide the one truth his child needed above all others?

Picking up the phone, he dialed Peyton's number. "Merry Christmas, Peyton," he said when she answered. "This is Matt Danville." How extraordinary that he should feel the need to introduce himself to the woman he was about to marry, that he couldn't simply expect her to recognize his voice. "I trust you've had a nice holiday."

"Yes, thank you," she replied, her voice soft with hesitation. "I hope yours was nice, as well."

"It was, yes, thank you," he said as if their stilted conversation was perfectly natural, completely normal. "Are you busy?"

"I'm packing, actually."

"Oh, that's right. You mentioned you were going to visit a friend in New Orleans."

"Baton Rouge," she corrected.

"Right. Baton Rouge." He gathered his courage, prepared to fling his reservations ahead of him off the cliffs of no return. "Can you…would you consider…canceling your trip?"

Her silence felt awkward, unencouraging. "Why do you ask?"

"I've been thinking." He cleared his throat. "Perhaps this would be a good time for us—for you and me—to make a trip to Niagara Falls."

"N-Niagara Falls?"

"Have you ever been there?"

"No. No, I thought it was a honeymoon resort."

He almost smiled. "A little more than that. The falls are spectacular…a natural wonder everyone should see at least once in a lifetime."

"You've been there?" she asked.

"Yes. But not on a honeymoon. I've never been married, Peyton. I thought there was a good possibility I would never marry." He paused before adding, "But then, you came along."

"I came along," she repeated, the words mocking his attempt to make this anything other than what it was—a contract into which neither of them wished to enter. "And what will we—you and I—do in Niagara Falls?"

Obviously, she wanted him to spell it out for her. "There are wedding chapels there, Peyton. We'll spend a couple of days in the area, get married, and be back in time to announce our marriage on New Year's Eve."

Her long sigh held regret and relief. "You agree with me, then, that this is the best alternative?"

"Yes. Have you changed your mind?"

"No, of course not but…you do think it's the right thing for us to do, Matt? I mean, we *are* virtual strangers."

"Who are going to have a child together."

"Who are going to have a child together," she repeated with deep resignation.

"I don't know if it's the right choice, Peyton. I have no idea if we're doing the right thing or if we're going to wish later that we'd done something else. But it's true that we live and work within a tightly knit, often highly judgmental community, and because of that, I believe marriage offers the best means of protecting you and the baby."

"It protects you, too, Matt. Please don't pretend you're only being noble."

He *was* being noble, damn it. She could allow him at least that much dignity. "Are you going to cancel your trip to Baton Rouge and come to Niagara Falls with me?" he asked tersely. "Or do you have another plan in mind?"

"No, you're right. If we're going to do this, an elopement is probably best. And the sooner, the better. It's not as if…as if waiting will make it easier."

The hint of tears in her voice elicited his reluctant sympathy. "Would you rather have a wedding here? With your family present?"

"Oh, no. No. An elopement is much more practical. And…safer."

Sure thing. As if her parents wouldn't be ecstatic about this union. He'd thought about that, too, during the past week. A lot. He knew there was a chance this situation had been orchestrated, or at least, encouraged, by her parents, who were eager to find acceptance within the society the Danvilles had been born into for generations. For Connie and Rick O'Reilly, this marriage would be the magic key they had made no secret of wanting for their daughters and for themselves. Matt was aware of the benefit the O'Reilly family would gain through this marriage. He'd given it due consideration. But in the end he'd decided it made no difference. He wasn't a victim in this. He'd made his choice and he would live with it. "Then we'll leave tomorrow morning," he said. "Shall I pick you up or would you prefer to meet somewhere?"

"The airport," she answered quickly. "I'll meet you there about ten. That's when I'd originally planned to arrive for my flight to Baton Rouge. I'll call my friend in Louisiana tonight and offer some excuse."

"Tell her you're eloping," Matt suggested. "I think we should try to be as honest as possible about what we're doing. We're the only ones who need ever know we're not in love and don't plan to stay married for the rest of our lives. Anything beyond that should be the truth, or as close to the truth as we can make it."

"I'm not sure there's any truth at all in this."

"Are you pregnant?"

"Yes. I would never lie about that."

"Then that's the only truth that counts."

"I don't know, Matt."

"You don't have to go through with this, Peyton. You can change your mind."

Her silence lasted so long he thought perhaps she had…and his heart inexplicably sank with regret. "I'll meet you at the airport," she replied resolutely. "At ten. Near the ticket counters."

"I'll find you."

"I'll make car rental and hotel reservations," she said in that take-charge voice he knew well.

"No, you just concentrate on breathing between now and tomorrow," he said. "I'll take care of the details." He hung up, took several long, deep breaths himself, then picked up the phone again to make the necessary arrangements.

PEYTON SANK onto the edge of her bed, letting the phone receiver dangle, the cord curl loosely through her fingers. *Breathe,* she thought. *Just breathe.*

But…*marriage.* Suddenly, it seemed so *real.*

She didn't know what she'd expected to feel, wasn't sure what she actually did feel now. Relief? Yes. She didn't want to face the pregnancy alone, not any part of it, good or bad. Remorse? Oh, yes, there was that, too. And much as she hated to admit it, she felt rescued. And grateful that he'd agreed to shoulder half the responsibility, for better or worse.

Of course, she'd known he couldn't do otherwise. She'd dealt with him on enough Foundation issues during the past several months to understand that he was a man of principle. Even when the principle he defended was wrong. She'd had enough arguments with him over the way the Foundation too often conducted its fund-raising to think he would shrink from a challenge. So why had she offered him such diametrically opposed, equally unpalatable, alternatives and then dared him to choose one over the other?

Because she'd thought maybe, somehow, that if she presented him such stark, black-and-white extremes, he would come up with a compromise. She'd hoped somehow he would see another option, the better idea that had eluded her. So now, it was settled.

They would marry. And she would keep breathing.

Admittedly, marriage would be a refuge from scandal and gossip. Having and raising a child alone, refusing to name the father, had not seemed an appealing prospect, although she would have done it if Matt's decision had been different, if circumstances had proved it necessary. Her mother would never have forgiven her. Connie Barton O'Reilly had been raised with an ideology that made illegitimacy a sin shared equally by mother and child; a baby born out of wedlock was a shameful mistake, a thing to be hidden, shunted into the background in order not to embarrass the entire family. Once she knew Matt Danville was the father, she would have moved heaven, earth and every cloud in between to force Peyton into marrying him. She would have used any means at her disposal to persuade Matt that marriage was the only honorable course. There would have been no trick too manipulative, no method too devious. Connie would have pulled out all the stops to have her daughter marry into one of the oldest, most honored families in New England.

Peyton knew this about her mother. She hated it, but she knew it. And she knew the damage it would cause. For Matt. For the baby. For Peyton, herself. Matt probably suspected it, too, and while she felt certain he wasn't happy about this solution, like her, he'd come to the conclusion that an elopement was their best hope of thwarting a scandal. She'd thought about this dilemma from every angle before she'd ever presented it to Matt. Now, he had reached the same conclusion.

And she was grateful.

Because no matter from which angle she looked at their situation, marriage seemed the lesser of the bad choices before them.

Replacing the phone on the bedside table, she turned to her suitcase, already packed, awaiting only her cosmetics bag and last-minute items. All she needed for a trip to Louisiana, but hardly anything warm enough for a trip to Niagara Falls in the dead of winter.

Eloping.

She was eloping.

"Hey, Pey." Scarlett tapped on the door and came in. "Can I borrow that sweater Mom gave you for Christmas? The blue one?"

Peyton hadn't even taken it out of the box. "I thought she got you one just like it."

Scarlett flounced onto the bed and began rifling through the suitcase. "Mine's pink. Pink would be much better for you. The blue would look much better on me. You know Mom, she never gets the colors right." She glanced up with a hopeful smile. "We could trade."

"I don't think your sweater will fit me."

"You should wear things tighter," Scarlett advised knowledgeably. "Show off your boobs. You've got 'em, why not flaunt 'em?"

Peyton picked the blue cashmere sweater out of her stack of gifts and tossed it to Scarlett, who caught it handily. "You can have mine and keep yours, as well," she said. "Just give me back that fleece pullover you stole a couple of weeks ago."

"Thanks." Scarlett smoothed the sweater, checked the attached tags. "I think I'll take this and the pink back and exchange them for this great pair of boots I saw at the mall. You don't mind, do you?''

''I don't.'' Peyton dumped out the contents of her suitcase, prepared to start over. ''Mom might.''

Scarlett watched with interest. ''She'll never notice. What are you doing?''

''Packing.'' In went two long-sleeved shirts and two sweaters. Peyton made a trip to the closet for wool slacks and a pair of jeans. From her dresser, she snatched heavy socks and a couple of long-sleeved tees and added them to the suitcase, too.

''I know it's December, Pey, but remember Louisiana is way south of here, and way warmer.''

''I haven't forgotten,'' she said, making room in the suitcase for her favorite flannel pj's.

Scarlett eyed the pajamas, then skewered Peyton with suspicion. ''Where are you going?'' she asked pointedly. ''Really.''

Peyton considered sticking with her original plan as alibi. Lying, in effect. ''Not to Louisiana,'' she hedged.

''That much I figured. Is this a recent itinerary change? Did you and Michelle decide to go skiing or something?''

''I'm not going to visit Michelle after all,'' Peyton said, then decided Matt was right about the truth. As much truth as possible. Scarlett would hate being the last to know. She might feel special knowing she was the first. "I'm going to Niagara Falls. To get married."

"Get out!" Scarlett laughed, falling back on the bed in a fit of giggles. "Like that's not the *biggest* lie you've *ever* told!"

"Maybe it's not a lie."

"Right." Sarcasm dripped from the word, bringing Scarlett back up to a sitting position beside the suitcase. "You're running off to get married. Ha. As if."

Peyton stayed mum. One good thing about a fifteen-year-old sister was that she could usually be counted on to argue all positions.

"Like, if you were *really* going to elope, you'd be packing flannel pajamas."

Good point. Peyton returned to the dresser, dug in her lingerie drawer until she found something more appropriate. A little black number made of silk so fine it looked like a gossamer cobweb—and as sexy as hell. She gave it a little flip before laying it in the suitcase, looked up in time to see Scarlett's jaw drop.

"You're just putting that in to trick me," Scarlett accused. "But I happen to know you haven't even been dating anyone, so how can you be getting married?"

"I imagine we'll stand before a minister and say, 'I do.'"

"All right, then, who's the guy?"

Peyton merely smiled. "You'll find out the minute we get back."

"That means this is all a joke." Scarlett flounced off the bed. "Well, it's not funny, Peyton. And I'm not giving you back the pullover, either. You'll have your new *husband* to keep you warm. So there!" She stalked out of the room then, taking the new blue sweater with her and slamming the door behind her as she went.

So much for truth, Peyton thought. But Scarlett was right about one thing.

Nothing about this was funny.

Not funny at all.

Chapter Four

"You may kiss the bride." The minister spoke matter-of-factly, nodding his head at the same time he closed his book with a satisfied thud, as if the sound carved one more notch on his belt of ceremonies successfully performed. He had an unfortunate nose, nearly three times the size of his tiny, receding chin, and hardly any upper lip, which made his broad smile resemble nothing so much as two toothy commas on either side of a thick exclamation point. "Congratulations," he said. "You're husband and wife."

"Thank you." Matt reached out to shake the man's hand, turned to smile his thanks at the woman who not only played the organ at the wedding chapel, acted as witness when called upon, filled out the paperwork, but also offered to be the vocalist, should the happy couple opt for an additional musical selection. Matt and Peyton had opted for the basic, no-frills wedding package and the music for their ceremony had consisted of a rather jazzy version of Wagner's "Wedding March" at the start, and what seemed to be a triumphant rendition of "We're Off to See the Wizard" at the end.

But Peyton might have been wrong about the last song. She'd be the first to admit she felt a little foggy at the moment and wasn't entirely certain of anything.

Except that she'd just married a man she barely knew. A man who'd skipped the traditional first kiss and done it so smoothly no one else seemed to have noticed.

Not that she was disappointed. No, indeed. This wasn't exactly a traditional wedding. Nor would it be a traditional marriage. And she certainly didn't expect a token kiss to mark its beginning. That would mean starting this strange relationship off with a lie and they had already agreed to be truthful with each other…no matter how *un*truthful they had to be in order to convince family and friends that theirs was a love match. So a kiss now was not required. Besides, the last time Matt kissed her— well, actually, it had been the first time—it had escalated from a keen curiosity between two consenting adults into a hotbed of passion between a man and a woman who, despite knowing that what they were doing was lunacy, still couldn't keep their hands—or lips—off each other.

What had happened at Matt's beach house had been a strange combination of attraction, a full moon, a higher than normal pitch of emotions, good wine, clandestine opportunity, and something Peyton couldn't quite put her finger on. Desire, maybe. Or a rebellion of sorts. Perhaps just the wrong combination at the right time.

Or maybe the right combination at the wrong time.

Any way she looked at it, though, *wrong* seemed to be the right description.

She didn't even want to think about it. Couldn't think about it. Remembering anything about that night provoked dangerous feelings.

Recalling Matt's seductive kiss and the response she hadn't even tried to deny brought the memories back in a tumble of emotions, made a jumble out of her rationalizations all over again. Safer to maintain their mutual, morning-after assurances to each other that they'd made a mistake. A huge mistake. A mistake they would simply forget ever happened.

Which, as it turned out, wasn't possible. So now that lapse in judgment had brought them to Niagara Falls and the White Dove Wedding Chapel and, possibly, probably, to yet another, even bigger, mistake.

"Right here!" The photographer snapped his fingers to get their attention and, like marionettes, they jerked around at the unexpected command. He raised his camera. "Now say, *'happily ever after!'*"

"Happ—" Peyton parroted without thinking, and that was the moment the shutter opened to catch her on film with her mouth agape, her expression startled, her single lily—what on *earth* had possessed her to choose to carry a lily of all possible bridal bouquets!—drooping limply in her hand. Her eyes were so wide and dazed by the flash that she looked more shell-shocked than bridal.

"IT'S NOT a *terrible* picture," Matt said reasonably, as if it wasn't clearly a complete waste of good film.

"Oh, please." Peyton sipped her water, glanced around the cozy pub-like restaurant and persistently avoided looking down at the vividly colored photograph. "Even if that ficus tree branch didn't appear to be growing out of the top of your head, and even if the artificial candlelight didn't cast us both in that weird greenish glow, you will never convince me that wayward pouf of baby's breath dangling over my head doesn't make me look like Frankenstein's bride."

He grinned at her and slid the offensive wedding photo off the table and into his jacket pocket. "If that's your charming Southern way of referring to me as Frankenstein's monster, I have to warn you, you're going to hurt my feelings.''

She smiled. Wanly. But a smile, just the same. ''If I'd wanted to hurt your feelings, Matt, I'd have called you a Yankee. You don't look half as awful in that picture as I do.''

''Except for the green lighting and the ficus tree.''

''Well, yes, except for that.'' She opened her menu, then closed it again. ''Do you think we could get rid of it?''

''The ficus tree or the lighting?''

''The whole photo.''

''Sure. I'll throw it away right now if you want.''

''Oh, no. We have to burn it.''

He glanced up from his menu, cocked his eyebrows. ''I didn't bring any matches.''

''You're making fun of me,'' she said and opened the menu again.

''I wouldn't do that, Peyton. Unless you called me a Yankee.'' His gaze returned to the menu. ''Now, what sounds good to you?''

''Mmm,'' she said as if considering. Her stomach wobbled a little at the thought of food. Or maybe she felt queasy over what she'd just done. *Married*. She'd actually *married* him. Of course, marriage is what she'd asked for, what she'd decided—and still believed—would be the best thing for all concerned, so it was a bit ridiculous to feel sick about it now that it was done.

He snapped shut the menu, smiled across the table at her. "I think I'll have the curried sea bass."

It was as if the words conjured the smells—the thick pungent spice of curry, the sea-salty scent of fish—and her stomach pitched like an angry surf. "Oh, jeez," she whispered, shoved back her chair and ran for the bathroom.

MATT KNEW how to handle women. He had two sisters, for one thing, so he'd been aware from an early age that females, for the most part, required special treatment. He'd learned young that girls were different, and that, on any given day, the same comment made the same way—with no underlying inflection or innuendo added—by the same brother, would elicit an entirely different response from the same sister. Sometimes, as best he'd ever been able to figure, simply because the sister in question did— or didn't—like her current haircut.

That early education in the ways of the opposite sex had stayed with him, and his opinion had changed very little over the years. He had dated a lot of women. He worked with a lot of women. A lot of smart, educated, ambitious women. He commanded a philanthropy that depended, to a significant degree, on his ability to cosset the matrons who volunteered their influence and largesse. He knew how best to keep his distance while discreetly flirting with the young wives who would one day be the matrons with influence and largesse. He knew how to flatter a woman's vanity, how to pamper her wounded pride, when to humor her disgruntled demands and when to put a stop to petty nonsense. He knew the value of listening and showing an appropriate amount of concern. He knew how to charm and cajole. He could be sympathetic or firm, unavailable or attentive, coaxing or casually indifferent, whatever he felt would best solve the problem. In short, he'd taken it as part of his job description to know when to compliment the haircut and when to keep his mouth shut. It had been a very long time since he'd run into a situation with a woman that he couldn't figure out how to handle.

Until now.

He'd known, of course, to get Peyton out of the restaurant as quickly and quietly as possible.

He'd known to get her into the car and start driving—not too fast, not too slowly, just smoothly and steadily—toward the house where they were staying. Thank goodness, he had friends in the area who had offered him the use of their home while they were away. Thank goodness, it was only about a twenty-minute drive. Thank goodness, Peyton was getting a bit of color back.

He'd figured out very quickly—after his first so-licitous ''How are you feeling?''—not to ask any more questions. She obviously wasn't in the mood to talk, with her head listing against the passenger-side window, her hands limp and pale in her lap. His suggestion that the seat could be made to recline met with a look that squelched further offers of as-sistance. She obviously wasn't in the mood for help-ful opinions or sympathetic gestures, either.

So he made none.

Once they'd traversed the long driveway and reached the house, he intended to go around, open her car door and offer a helping hand into the house, but she was out of the car before him and ahead of him going up the porch steps. The second he'd un-locked the front door, she'd pushed it open, run to the bathroom and locked herself inside. He'd fol-lowed, waiting in the hallway in case she needed help, although he was certain she'd rather suffer than unlock that door and ask for his assistance. But he didn't know what else to do, so he hovered there in the hallway, feeling guilty for no reason and help-less for more reasons than he could name. In a few minutes, he heard the thunder of water sluicing from the tap and into the tub and smelled the first fragrant burst of bath salts. Apparently, she planned to stay in there for a good long while.

Not exactly the way he'd pictured his wedding night.

Of course, calling it a wedding night was a misnomer. And thinking of it that way was…well, dangerous. Peyton didn't feel well. At the restaurant, her skin had turned as pale as milk in a matter of seconds. All the way home, she'd looked fragile, shaky, and so vulnerable, he ached to take her in his arms and reassure her that she wasn't in this alone, that somehow, it would all turn out right.

But, of course, he wasn't sure it would turn out all right. And touching her would be…well, dangerous. Because she didn't want to be touched. And because touching could be so easily misinterpreted as something more than it was. And because he wanted to start out their relationship with as few complications as possible.

Which was about the dumbest thought he'd ever had. Their relationship was a complication. It was nothing but complications. Period. There was simply no other way to describe it.

The sound of rushing water stopped as abruptly as it had begun, but steam seeped beneath the door, filling the hallway with the heated scent of bath salts, and an alluring, almost suffocating sense of intimacy. Matt stood, like a voyeur, listening to the splash as Peyton eased into the water, hearing, or imagining he heard, the slow, soft sigh she released as the fragrant warmth enveloped her body.

Her naked body.

He turned abruptly, taming by sheer willpower the embarrassing rush of heat that had coursed through him in a whirlwind of unasked-for, unanticipated desire. What was wrong with him, anyway? Standing in the hallway, listening to Peyton getting into a bath. Imagining her there. Imagining—even for only an instant—getting into the bath with her, doing things he felt ashamed to admit he could even think about at a time like this.

She was pregnant. She was sick. She'd just married a damn Yankee.

Thinking of this marriage in any other terms, remembering even the smallest details about the night and the passion that had gotten them here was…well, dangerous.

So he walked down the hall and into the bedroom where he'd earlier placed her suitcase. His, of course, was in a bedroom on the other side of the house. There was a lot to be said for the layout of this house and the privacy it afforded. No one would ever know they'd spent their first nights as husband and wife on opposite ends of the house. Exactly what he'd had in mind when he'd called Rob and asked to use the house. He hadn't wanted to stay at a hotel where they'd share a room for the sake of appearance. That would have been difficult, at best, and he'd wanted Peyton to feel comfortable on this odd honeymoon.

Or at least no more uncomfortable than could be helped.

So, this arrangement had turned out just the way he'd planned it.

Which was about the only thing today that had gone the way he'd planned. The wedding chapel wasn't as it had been pictured in the brochure and, in daylight, appeared to be on the shabby side of respectability. The organ music had sounded tinny and off-key. The flowers, except for Peyton's single lily, had been artificial and muted with dust. And Matt had stood there, repeating the minister's words, trying to focus on the seriousness of what he and Peyton were doing, and the only thing he could think of was that the man had the biggest nose he'd ever seen.

Not what he'd ever imagined he would be thinking about during his wedding.

But then, he'd never actually imagined himself getting married.

Walking back down the hall, holding his breath as he passed the bathroom door so he wouldn't catch the scent of the bath salts again, he walked straight to the front door and outside. The December air felt icy cold in his lungs and chilled him through, but the night was clear and bright with stars. He stayed outside on the porch for several long minutes, just breathing in and watching the exhaled air float up toward the stars. Then he jumped the steps and jogged over to lock the rental car. Noticing Peyton's lily lying cold and forgotten on the dash, he retrieved it and carried it inside. He found a vase in the kitchen and sank the stem as far as it would go into warm water. The lily seemed to perk up almost immediately, so maybe the rest of the evening could be salvaged to some extent as well.

His original plan for after the ceremony—dinner out, a drive across the Rainbow Bridge to view the falls at night, then a leisurely return to the house, set in its dark, sleepy vineyard—hadn't come off as he'd imagined, either. He'd thought that after a big meal and a long drive, they'd both be tired enough to talk only a little and then go to their separate bedrooms, hopefully already a bit closer to the friendship they'd each said they wanted this marriage to become.

That had been a good plan.

Except that Peyton was in the bathtub, soaking her squeamish tummy, and he was not only keyed up, colder than an icicle, but starving. The curried sea bass was nothing but a tantalizing thought that made his stomach clench with hunger. Opening the refrigerator, he smiled, thankful Miranda wasn't the only one of the Danvilles who could plan ahead. He'd asked Evelyn and Rob—this was, after all, their house and vineyard—if they'd give him the name of someone local who would stock the house for him before his and Peyton's arrival. They'd told him not to worry, they'd take care of it, and they'd obviously done more than simply instruct someone to get a few groceries. There was wine, champagne, juice, mixers, all kinds of fruit, an assortment of cheese, crackers, chilled, cooked shrimp with cocktail sauce and various covered dishes, marked with instructions and ready for the oven. Reaching for the one marked Veal Scallopini he remembered Peyton's reaction to the mere mention of food at the restaurant and decided maybe he should avoid putting anything in the oven and thereby unleashing smells that might upset her stomach all over again.

Crackers. Hadn't Miranda always insisted the twins eat plain crackers when they'd had a touch of stomach upset? And cheese? Hadn't he read somewhere that milk products were soothing for stomach ailments? It sounded reasonable, so he put together a tray of cheese and crackers, debated about the shrimp, but there again, it *was* fish. So he settled on just the crackers and cheese, poured himself a glass of wine, and got a bottle of mineral water for Peyton.

He added the lone lily in its crystal vase to the

tray and carried it carefully into the other room. It took a few minutes to rearrange the logs already stacked in the fireplace, but only a small adjustment to the gas to get a nice fire blazing behind the screen. He crouched there for a few minutes, soaking in the warmth and feeling rather proud of the accomplishment, as he didn't, ordinarily, have occasion to light a fire. Or fix a tray of food, for that matter. It occurred to him how privileged his whole life had been. Unless he counted the seemingly constant absence of his parents.

His child would not feel that lack. Ever. Matt was determined to be there for his son or daughter. No matter what sacrifice he had to make. Had already made.

Married. He was married.

By now, Ainsley, Miranda and Andrew would know. He'd sent them each a note, stating that he'd eloped with Peyton O'Reilly, that he'd fill them in on all the happy details later, that they could expect to greet their new sister-in-law on New Year's Eve, but until then, he'd appreciate a little privacy. He knew his siblings. They'd be dying to dial his cell phone, but they'd respect his request.

He wasn't so sure what the O'Reillys would do when they received the note he'd written to Rick. Peyton didn't know about that. Not yet. But Matt had felt, as a gentleman, it was his responsibility to inform her parents of the elopement. He'd sent word to his parents as well, although it could be days before they received the message. All in all, he felt he'd done everything he could to smooth the path ahead for Peyton, soften the surprise, and give the impression that their elopement might have been impulsive but not unplanned.

He breathed her in—the fragrances of bath and woman wrapped around one another in a subtle, intoxicating scent—even before he heard the scuff of her feet against the carpet and looked up to see her. She stood just inside the room, a white robe swaddling her from ankle to chin, the fleecy lapels folding back to reveal a small vee of creamy breastbone and framing the slender curve of her neck. Her hair was damp and curly, caught up on top of her head with a clip that left tendrils twirling loosely about her nape, spiraling around her face. She had her hands nestled inside the long sleeves, had one sleeve tucked cozily inside the other, like a chenille muff. Her feet were bare and her face, too, wore only the rosy warmth of a hot bath.

His heart caught, beat once, skipped another beat, then settled again into a steady rhythm. In all his planning, he hadn't once imagined her looking like this. Or that he would feel such a surge of pure, melting temptation in the simple tilt of the smile that graced her prettily bowed lips.

"A fire," she said as if it were an extraordinary thing. "I love fires in December."

"As opposed to fires in other months?" he asked, smiling, too.

"Winter isn't particularly cold in Louisiana, so I never even lived in a house with a fireplace until we moved north. But when I was a little girl, every year a couple of days before Christmas, Dad would put up this cardboard setup—for Santa, you know—and I'd pretend the flames were real and gather my dolls and stuffed animals in front of it so they'd be warm while I conducted these elaborate Christmas tea parties." The slight dip of her chin apologized for the nostalgia. "After December, the cardboard fireplace went back to the attic, the dolls went back on the shelf, and I went back to coloring pictures at my little table in the restaurant while Mom and Dad worked."

He turned to the fire, wary of the heat he was feeling in just looking at her, cautious of his sudden empathy with the lonely child she had been. "Are you feeling better?" he asked, pushing to his feet, away from the warmth.

"Much," she said brightly. "Is there anything to eat?"

He gestured at the coffee table and the tray. "I brought a bottle of mineral water for you, but if you'd rather have some tea or broth, I'll make some."

"Tea or broth," she repeated, her nose crinkling in dismay. "I was hoping for something a little more…substantial."

"Well, there's plenty of crackers."

"Crackers," she repeated, nose still wrinkled.

"And cheese," he quickly added.

"And cheese."

"You don't like cheese?"

"I do," she hastened to assure him. "It's just that… Please don't misunderstand. I love this house, tucked in its little vineyard, and it was super nice of your friends to let us use it while they're away and I really am glad we aren't staying in a hotel…"

"But…?"

Her shoulder lifted in a tiny shrug. "But right now I so wish we could call room service."

"You're hungry?"

"Starving." She bent down and snagged a sesame-seed cracker, nibbled at the edge, then, for some reason, dropped the rest of it into the robe's deep pocket. "I guess there isn't a lot of food in the house, though. Tomorrow, maybe, we should go to a grocery store and stock up."

"Stock up." Now she had him repeating words. "If we had room service and you could order anything you wanted, what would it be?"

A dreamy look came into her eyes. "Mmm. Spring rolls, or maybe lettuce wraps for starters. Turtle soup…definitely. And bread, preferably sour-dough. Then something with pasta…linguine, maybe. In red clam sauce."

"Not white clam sauce," he clarified, amazed at this transformation in her appetite.

"I prefer red."

"No dessert?"

She hesitated, dropped her chin. "I was thinking ice cream…and a piece of apple pie. Maybe a straw-berry milk shake, too. Oh, and bread pudding. White-chocolate bread pudding."

Now *he* was starting to feel a little sick. "Are you sure—?" He stopped himself mid-sentence, because it seemed almost about as bad to mention her earlier state of distress as to ignore it. "You'll be pleased to learn there is more substantial food in the refrig-erator. Unless you think you'd be wiser to stick with just crackers and cheese."

She was gone before the last words were out of his mouth, and he heard the pad of her feet on the tile of the kitchen floor. "Wow," she said as the refrigerator door suctioned open. "Did *you* do this, Matt?" she called.

He downed his glass of wine in one long swallow before he followed her to the kitchen and stopped in the doorway. "No. The food is compliments of

Evelyn and Rob. I did ask them to have someone stock a few groceries for us, but they, obviously, felt we'd require a little more sustenance than I originally had in mind.''

She went on surveying the contents of the fridge. ''There's veal scallopini in here. And lasagna. And Cornish hens. And croissants. And two or three kinds of salad. And fruit and…oh, my…'' Her voice faded into a nearly orgasmic sigh as she shuffled dishes. ''Someone's made a clam sauce. I bet there's linguine around here someplace.''

''*Red* clam sauce?''

''White,'' she answered. ''My favorite.'' With that contradiction, she lifted her head and teased him with her smile over the refrigerator door. ''Exactly how long is this honeymoon going to last, anyway?''

''Seven months plus one year,'' he replied without thinking…and was immediately sorry when the teasing smile vanished.

''Let me rephrase,'' she said pointedly. ''How long are we staying here?''

''I thought we'd go home late afternoon on the thirty-first, and make our big announcement that night at the New Year's Eve party at Nate's coffeehouse, although I suspect everyone will know by then, anyway.''

''Let's eat some of this shrimp.'' She pulled the

bowl from the shelf and closed the refrigerator door with a bump from her hip. She had a good-size pink shrimp halfway to her lips, when she stopped cold, offered up a rather startled look. "What do you mean, *everyone* will know by then?"

"News like this travels fast, Peyton. Ainsley has always had trouble keeping a secret. And with something this exciting, I expect Miranda will be just about as bad. They may have the news spread all the way to the Atlantic seaboard by the time we get home. I certainly expect it will be all over Newport."

"You *told* your sisters we were eloping? And…and they *believed* you?"

"I didn't tell them, Peyton. I wrote notes." He paused. "Why wouldn't they believe me?"

Color heightened in her cheeks. "I thought we'd agreed not to say anything until we were married."

"And *I* thought we'd agreed to pretend that this elopement was a romantic impulse."

"*After* the fact. How can we say it was an impulse when you told everyone before it even happened? The whole point of an elopement is the element of surprise."

"The whole *point* of an elopement is to get married. And I didn't tell everyone. I wrote notes to my sisters and brother, and one to each set of parents."

"You wrote a note to my *parents?*"

Grabbing control of his rising frustration, he crossed the room, poured himself another glass of wine and swallowed a third of it in one quaff. It had been one hell of a day. "I wrote to your father, actually, to apologize for stealing off with his daughter and bypassing the formality of asking for her hand in marriage, but assuring him that we were crazy in love and couldn't wait to be wed."

The bloom in her cheeks took on a temperamental heat. "You actually wrote the words *crazy in love* and *couldn't wait to be wed?* To my father?"

He focused on not crushing the stem of the glass as he sucked down another third of his drink. It was a very good wine and deserved more careful enjoyment. Unfortunately, frustration zapped that pleasure, too. "I don't remember the exact way I worded it, but something to that effect, yes."

Tossing the solitary shrimp back into the bowl, she ducked into the fridge and came out with a bottle of apple juice. "You know, when I found out I was pregnant, I didn't think giving up alcohol would be any great sacrifice. I realize now I could be wrong, and I think it's very rude of you to be drinking that wine in front of me. If I have to give up even an occasional glass, you should have to, too." A thrust of her left hip closed the door for the second time and she marched out of the room, the bowl of shrimp in one hand, the bottle of juice in the other, and her chin so high it was a wonder she could see where she was going.

This Peyton he recognized, although he wasn't clear about just what he'd done to bring about her return. He did, however, very purposefully refill his glass before he went after her. "I didn't want your family thinking something bad had happened when you didn't arrive in Baton Rouge as planned. There's no cause to worry them unnecessarily. Writing a note was the reasonable, proper thing to do."

"Proper. Now there's a good word." She flounced onto the sofa, the robe falling apart above her knees, exposing a flash of inner thigh, a length of lovely, long leg, which was immediately tucked up beneath her and the robe adjusted over it. But he'd had a glimpse…and his skin remembered the silky feel, the smooth, heated texture of her legs tangled up with his. She gave the robe a last flick of modesty. "I'm surprised, Matt, you didn't use *that* word in your reasonable note."

She was being completely unreasonable, maddeningly petulant. Which meant he should remain calm and not allow her to goad him into further argument. So, he took the chair opposite her and sipped his wine as he watched her dunk a shrimp into cocktail sauce and then pop it into her mouth. "Are you upset because I wrote a note to your family or because I didn't use the word *proper* in it?"

She discarded the chitinous tail onto the tray and reached for another shrimp. "I can't decide. Maybe I'm upset because you took it upon yourself to inform my family about our elopement without telling me. Or maybe it's the idea that I now have to convince my dad we are *crazy in love*. Or *maybe* it's because you always do what's *proper,* Matt, and sometimes that's just a little hard for me to handle."

"Oh, come on, Peyton. You know as well as I do how hard it is to ensure something like this remains a secret. Someone could have seen us together at the airport. The clerk at the license bureau might have recognized our names. I didn't want to take a chance on our families hearing about our marriage because of some obscure coincidence. I thought the news should come from me. I thought you'd be relieved not to have to spring this news on your family out of the blue. I *thought* it would give you a little more time to get used to the idea yourself before you had to talk to them about it."

"Oh, well, thank you so *much,* Matt. But as it happens, you have just opened up a whole can of Louisiana worms!"

"You can still call and tell them yourself. There's a working phone right over there." He indicated the phone with a nod. "Call them right now."

"No, thank you. I don't want to call them now.

I don't want to call them later. I don't want to call them at all.''

It had been a stressful day. He tried to keep that in mind as he wrestled with the desire to tell her she wasn't making any sense. And he was finding that increasingly hard to handle. ''Would you rather your family found out you're married from some gossipy busybody who knows someone who knows someone else who may have heard it from God knows who?''

''Yes,'' she said. ''Yes, as a matter of fact, I would.''

Frustration made him down the rest of his wine in a single swallow. ''You're not thinking clearly about this, Peyton.''

''My thinking is perfectly clear, thank you.'' She leveled a shrimp at him. ''*I'm* not the one drinking.''

He was tempted to go back for a refill just to spite her, but he saw no reason to court a hangover simply because she seemed determined to aggravate him. Fortunately, he was just as determined to maintain his composure. ''Okay, Peyton, why don't you explain to me how you think our families should find out we're married?''

She eyed him critically as she sucked another shrimp into her mouth and discarded the tail, wiping her fingertips on the napkin, then dabbing at the corners of her mouth. ''By osmosis,'' she said. ''Or—

here's a thought—we could have told them *to-gether.*''

"After the fact."

"Well, of course, *after* the fact. Telling them beforehand defeats the purpose."

Seven months, plus one year, was beginning to look like a very long time. "The purpose of eloping? Or the purpose of telling them?"

"Both. Neither. I don't know. You're only trying to confuse me."

He couldn't help but smile. "How am I doing?"

"It's not funny," she insisted.

"I understand that, Peyton, and it will be even less funny if we start off our marriage arguing over which way we should have informed our families."

The current shrimp landed back in the bowl and she leaned forward to set the bowl on the tray, showing more cleavage than she meant to, and more than enough to distract his tenuous composure. "I just didn't want my mother to have too much lead time," she said, settling forward on the edge of the cushion. "You don't have any idea what we're in for."

"It can't be worse than if she heard about this at the beauty shop or down at the deli."

Peyton sighed and stood up, wrapping the robe tighter around her. "I know this doesn't really fit with your idea of *proper*, Matt, but please, believe me. My mother would be utterly thrilled if she had heard about our marriage from the man behind the counter at the deli.''

''That is a little hard to believe.'' His smile met a cool lift of her eyebrow and he quickly tucked it out of sight.

She cinched the tie belt with another hard tug. ''The only thing my mother would have loved more is if she could have planned a huge, showy splash of a wedding. I've cheated her out of that by eloping and now you've taken away the huge satisfaction she would have received from never letting me forget that she had to learn about my marriage from some totally unsuitable person.''

''Don't you think you're being a little unfair to her, Peyton?''

Her response was simply a pitying look. ''I seem to have lost my appetite, so I think I'll just go on to bed. It's been a long day.''

He stood, afraid she was feeling ill again, afraid she was having second thoughts, afraid she wasn't. ''Good idea,'' he said. ''Sleep late in the morning, if you want. I thought we might drive over to the butterfly sanctuary in the afternoon, see if it's open.''

''Okay. If it's not snowing.''

God help him if it did snow and trapped him in this house alone with her all day. And the next day. And the day after that. They'd either be fighting like cats and dogs or… Even the thought of what followed that "or" was…well, dangerous. "If it's not snowing," he repeated brightly. "Good night, Peyton."

"Good night, Matt."

He watched her walk away and realized his appetite had vanished, too. Too much wine, probably. But he thought he'd have another glass, just the same. One he could enjoy in front of the fire. Alone.

Which was not exactly the way he'd planned to spend his wedding night.

PEYTON SAT on the edge of the bed and pushed her toes in and out of the fuzzy slippers. Matt's friends had provided every luxury, from the fleecy robe to the slippers to the silky cotton sheets to the plethora of rich food in the kitchen. She'd lied to Matt about her appetite and she really wished she had some of that food now. Her stomach growled with hunger. Which seemed to be the way pregnancy affected her. Either nausea or an appetite of gargantuan proportions. There didn't seem to be any room for compromise.

The news that he'd sent her parents a note—*a note!*—should have stripped away the desire to do anything but strangle him. Her mother was probably in hog heaven by now, plotting some extravagant and overblown reception or regaling her friends and family with woeful accounts of her daughter's inconsiderate behavior. Peyton knew she could pick up the phone and call them, but what would that accomplish, except making her feel worse? And letting them know she had nothing better to do on her wedding night than explain why she had chosen to elope.

No. She wouldn't call and she couldn't leave the bedroom without having to explain to Matt that her appetite was running amok. Pushing up from the bed, she walked to the window, checked to see if it was snowing. She didn't know what she and Matt would do tomorrow if it snowed.

Well, okay, so her imagination was running amok as well, producing ideas that were, obviously, not on his agenda. He was in his bedroom. She was in hers. Which was exactly as it should be. She supposed.

Her stomach rumbled again and she turned from the window to consider the bed. Jamming her hands into the pockets of her robe, she found a cracker and looked at it curiously. The evening was looking up. She'd get into bed and nibble on the cracker while she read the mystery novel she'd brought along.

It wasn't the way she'd ever imagined spending her wedding night, true, but it wasn't as bad as lying in bed alone, thinking about her husband lying alone in his bed thinking about her.

Or sleeping soundly and not thinking about her at all.

Which was even more depressing than wondering how one solitary cracker was going to put a dent in her appetite.

Chapter Five

"Andy?" Ainsley knocked on the door of Andrew's studio as she opened it and stepped inside. "Andrew?"

Crash! Thump, thump, thump, thump, thump!

Startled by the noise, Ainsley jumped back and looked to her right, where a pair of feet in spanking-white socks extended from beneath a tree. Actually, it was a painting of a tree. A backdrop. On top of a gray-swirled backdrop. On top of a blue-splotched backdrop. On top of about ten other backdrops. Normally, they hung on wide rods. Andrew used them for portrait work, pulling down one backdrop in front of another, or rolling them up as necessary to get the background he wanted for a picture.

Now they were all in a pile on the polished wood floor on top of someone, who could only be Andrew's assistant. "Hayley?" Ainsley stooped down and addressed the painted tree. "Are you all right?"

"I'm fine," Hayley's voice sang out, muffled but cheery. The backdrops shifted as she began wiggling out from beneath them. Gradually, a pair of drab olive pants appeared, the folds of the material emphasizing that they were too large for the long legs and narrow hips they covered. The waistband was cinched tight with a seventies-style macramé belt. With red wooden beads woven in with the ecru threads. Next, the smooth planes of a sleek belly appeared, a silver ring looped through the navel to add interest. A moment later, Hayley emerged in full and in all her baggy splendor.

Ainsley watched as Hayley's trademark T-shirt fell down to conceal the curves of a slim, athletic body, the silver belly button ring and the macramé belt. Unfortunately, the parts Hayley routinely kept covered weren't—in Ainsley's opinion—the part that needed to be kept out of sight. Her hairstyle was a disaster. Her vivid red hair had been braided so tightly, the individual coils spiraled and sprung in all directions, giving a whole new meaning to the term *dreadlocks*.

"Need some help?" Ainsley extended a hand to Hayley.

"Thank goodness, it's only you. I thought it was Andrew coming through the door." Hayley got to her feet and dusted herself off. She patted her T-shirt pocket, pulled out a pair of overlarge black-framed glasses and stuck them on her face. She looked like a raccoon in a wig. "He said he wouldn't be back until after lunch," she said. "But sometimes—a lot of times, lately—he changes his mind and comes in when he said he wouldn't. I never know when he's going to show up." She cast a sheepish glance from behind the camouflaging black glasses. "And you know how that rattles me."

Ainsley sighed. "You have to stop being intimidated by him, Hayley. For heaven's sake, he's just a guy."

"Easy for you to say. He's your brother. He can't fire you."

"He's not going to fire you, Hayley. I've told you that a hundred times. If he didn't like your work, he wouldn't have kept you on as his assistant for the past nine months."

"Ten," Hayley said. "It's been ten months since he hired me."

"I can't even remember the last time he managed to hold on to an assistant for longer than four months. See? You're already a fixture in the studio."

"Only because I do the work and I clean up after myself. I could bring in a trained chimpanzee as a substitute and Andrew would never notice the difference."

Ainsley laughed. "That isn't true, and you know it."

A reluctant smile crept into Hayley's green eyes and curved the corners of her mouth. "All right, so maybe he'd pay *some* attention." She brushed at her clothes again and looked helplessly at the jumble of backdrops. "But he'll always think of me as a klutz."

For months now, since the first time she'd heard her brother mention his new assistant, Ainsley had been studying Hayley, getting to know her and like her very much, despite the insecurities that drove Andrew nuts. It hadn't taken long for Ainsley to discover that Hayley had a huge crush on Andrew...and it didn't take much imagination to see the possibility that something more could develop, given the proper circumstances. For a couple of months now, Ainsley had offered broad hints that there were things a matchmaker could do to help level the playing field at the studio. Hayley didn't have to feel ignored. She didn't need to feel like a klutz. She could do something about the situation.

But the hints produced no perceptible change. It was time to step in and do something drastic, Ainsley decided. "He knows how talented you are, Hayley. He's told me. I know he's told you. Maybe you ought to try believing what he says for a change."

Hayley shook her head. "He just says that to be nice. So I won't quit."

"Why don't you quit if you're so rattled by him?"

"Well, because…" Hayley looked as if the idea was ridiculous and the answer obvious. "I'd never quit. He's the most talented, most experienced, most artistic, most wonderful man—I mean, *photographer*—in the world. And he's teaching me so much I could never learn from anyone else. I'd be an idiot to walk away from this opportunity."

"Plus, you have an enormous crush on him."

Hayley's shoulders sagged. "There's that, too."

It was definitely time for action. "Come on." Ainsley took the other woman's arm. "I have an idea."

"Where are we going?"

"To a New Year's Eve party."

"Now? It's not even ten in the morning yet."

"Tonight, but we have a lot of work to do between now and then."

Hayley balked. "Oh, I couldn't leave the studio."

"You're taking today off."

"But…"

"No buts. You need a makeover to give you confidence and I'm giving you one. My treat." Ainsley steered her toward the door. "We are going to have a wonderful day and tonight Andrew will be the one who gets rattled when you walk in.''

"He is?'' Hayley resisted, but only a little. "I don't see how that could happen.''

"You will,'' Ainsley the matchmaker said. "Trust me. I know what I'm doing.''

"YOU MET MICHELLE in second grade,'' Matt said, driving as effortlessly as he seemed to do most things, glancing occasionally in the rearview mirror, occasionally at Peyton. "And she's been your best friend ever since. Her last name is…Trierre, and your nickname for her is…'' He frowned, his profile clean-cut and aristocratic, the classic angles of forehead, nose, jaw and chin combining years of good genetics with strong character and confidence. "Why can't I remember that?''

Peyton laid her head against the headrest and closed her eyes, wishing she had never suggested they go over all this again. Actually, she wished she'd never made it into a game they'd played over the course of the honeymoon. *Tell me the name of your best friend. Nicknames the other kids called you. Your first true memory. Aunts. Uncles. Cousins. Favorite teacher when you were a child. Your favorite music group in high school. Music you listen to now. First book you ever read more than once. Happiest childhood memory. Most embarrassing moment.* Details of their lives, past and present, little things that a newly married couple would know about each other, that would lend credence to their concocted story of all the dates they'd had, the time they'd spent together before this impulsive but so romantic elopement. No matter how seemingly insignificant or unimportant, Peyton had tried to cover all the bases, knowing it was often the tiniest nothing in conversation that brought down a house of cards. "Collie," she said with feigned patience. "I called her Collie. Shel, short for Michelle. T, her last initial. Shel-T. Sheltie. Which is a dog that looks like—"

"—a small collie. Right." Matt nodded, apparently convinced he wouldn't have trouble with that one again. "And she called you Pug." He took his eyes off the highway long enough to glance at her again. "Because…?"

"Because I called her Collie first and the first breed she thought of that started with a P was—"

"Pug." He grinned broadly, pleasurably.

She didn't have to open her eyes to see it. His enjoyment of this particular part of her past was already well documented in her memory. She had already warned him that Michelle was the *only* person who would ever *dare* call her by the nickname. It was private. Between friends. Which didn't seem to bother him, or keep him from going over the story again and again...as if he couldn't quite keep it straight.

"Well, at least she didn't call you Pekinese. Or Poodle."

"I think I'd have made a great poodle." She moved her shoulder restlessly beneath the seat restraint, hoping they were close to home, dreading the actual moment they'd arrive as well as the evening ahead. "Now that you have my first experience with nicknames mapped in your brain, maybe we could turn on the radio and listen to music."

"Oh, I think we need to keep practicing," he said, trying, without much success, to sound quite serious. "Tonight's the big test, you know."

"Great. Nothing like a little added pressure."

"We're probably ten minutes out. Still time for a pop quiz."

He was enjoying this. Or the idea of going home. Probably that, since it meant the pretense of the honeymoon lay behind them. Now all they had to do was get through the next seven months plus one year of pretending they were married. Well, they *were* married. Just not truly married. Except she had to stop thinking of it that way. Now—tonight, in fact— they were going to face the family and friends who, if they didn't know about the elopement already from Matt's proper notes—soon would get the news in person. She wished she could feign illness, or at least a queasy stomach and stay home, but she wasn't one to hide from unpleasant tasks. And, in truth, she'd already used the nausea associated with pregnancy as an excuse more than once during the past few days when the intimacy of being alone with Matt sent her thoughts along paths they had no business going. Besides, the sooner they got through this first celebratory event, the easier it would be to fall comfortably into the lie.

At least, that was the theory.

"Ask me something," he prodded. "Anything."

"Are you positive you've never had a nickname?"

"Absolutely certain. At least, none that I remember. But then, I didn't meet my best friend until college, and by that time, nicknames seemed a little juvenile. The family still calls Ainsley Baby, though, and on occasion, if Miranda's really mad at me, she'll refer to me as The Jonathan. But since Jonathan is part of my name, I don't think it counts as a true nickname."

"Scarlett sometimes calls me Pey. But then, she's at that age where two syllables often qualify as a conversational commitment, so I'm not sure it really counts as a nickname, either."

"Guess we're stuck with Pug, then."

He was enjoying this a little too much, in her

opinion. "Don't give up, Matt. I may come up with a nickname for you, yet."

His laugh came out throaty rich, deep and sensual, sending a quiver of awareness, unimpeded, down her spine. "I think I'll call you Sweet Pea when the moment requires an endearment. Doesn't that have a certain Southern flair?"

He changed lanes, deftly, efficiently, and yet the motion bothered Peyton, made her feel a twist of queasiness, an unease she'd been fighting ever since they'd arrived back in Rhode Island. She opened her eyes, saw they were approaching the Newport Bridge, which spanned Narragansett Bay in a sweep of engineering grace and beauty. Her stomach contracted with renewed dread. They'd be at Danfair in a matter of minutes. Ten. Fifteen. And then the real charade would begin.

"I think I'm going to be sick."

His concern was palpable. It enveloped her and made her feel as if he could protect her from whatever lay ahead, which was ridiculous. "I didn't think it was *that* bad," he said. "But if you really don't like Sweet Pea, I'll think of something else."

She managed a smile, grateful that he didn't swamp her with solicitous questions. Of course, during the past few days, she'd rejected his every attempt to aid her during the "morning" sickness which, for her, obviously, wasn't confined to the a.m. hours. She'd turned down his offers of Chamomile tea and bland crackers; she'd turned away from his sincerely offered sympathy because she knew that, however well intended, accepting any comfort at all from him would create a breach in her defenses, giving him license to ask personal questions and offer his opinion or advice.

She wasn't ready to share the pregnancy with him. Not yet. Not when it meant talking about changes in her body that were still elusive and a little startling even to her. At some point, maybe it wouldn't matter anymore. At some point, maybe this hormonal swing would stop playing havoc with her emotions. At some point, maybe she'd need his understanding and his help. But not yet. Not now. She scrunched her shoulders, stretched the taut muscles across her neck, then relaxed and exhaled the stress.

"Okay again?"

"Yes, thanks." She had an odd impulse to reach over and pat his hand—his large, shapely man's hand resting on the console between them—to reassure him that he didn't need to worry about her. But, of course, she didn't. Touching him, even accidentally, sparked an electric flash of attraction, a burning beneath her skin. Just the thought of it flooded her with hot desire. *Sexual* desire. Why hadn't pregnancy affected *that,* along with her appetite and emotions? "I'm just a little nervous," she said, as if that came within a yard of describing her restlessness. "About tonight."

"Don't be. I'll handle the announcement. The only thing you'll have to do is collect good wishes and look happy."

She let her head roll to the left and caught the edge of his smile. "Thank you, Matt."

"For what? Being the guy who gets congratulated and slapped on the back? Or for deflecting all that glory off of you?"

He was a nice man, she thought, and he was trying very hard to make the best of a bad situation. "For being considerate," she said, "and kind and more patient with me than I deserved."

His gaze swept over her, intensely blue and direct. "We're in this together, Peyton. You're going to be the mother of my child. I think that deserves special consideration."

The mother of his child. For the first time, the thought brought a whisper of excitement that lingered and promised to stay. They had created a new life. However much she regretted the circumstances, she wanted this baby, loved it wondrously, protectively already. And she felt glad Matt was the father. He was a good man, a gentleman, one of those powerful, solid men who believed in family honor and doing the right thing. He would be a good father, and that would be a good thing for her child. She had to count herself lucky that her first taste of desperate, out-of-control passion had been with this man and not someone far less...perfect.

"Tell me something you regret," she asked impulsively. "Something other than...this."

They were turning off Farewell Street and onto Spring. Danfair was only a few blocks away. Matt knew the neighborhood, had lived here all his life and she realized his silence wasn't concentration. It lasted long enough to be uncomfortable, to make her wish she hadn't asked the question. "I'm the Jonathan of my generation," he said. "Being born to that sort of privilege doesn't allow much room for regrets."

So there it was. Peyton heard the undertone of self-loathing in his voice, knew this marriage would be his great regret. Oh, he'd never admit it—not to her—and she had no doubt he'd treat her with kindness, patience and due consideration. But he'd never be able to look at her without feeling he'd betrayed his family and his heritage.

And she would never look at him without knowing she'd betrayed herself.

The mansions of Newport surrounded them now, scrolling past the car windows in all their glory, some gated and closed, some open to the public, all of them magnificent examples of architecture and opulence from the glory days of the Vanderbilts and the Gilded Age of sumptuous wealth. Danfair was one of the oldest *cottages,* as these summerhouses had once been called, and for the next nineteen months, it would be her home.

Her mother must be in a state of wicked glee and agitated delight by now. She was probably beside herself with excitement and plans for how to amplify her daughter's coup into the one thing she, herself, had always craved…personal status. Connie had been born as far from this life as it was possible to get: from a shabby trailer on the wrong side of the bayou, she'd clawed her way out of poverty, married a man with malleable ambitions and worked beside him from dawn to midnight, pushing, prodding and plotting to create the wealth she believed would bring her everything she'd ever wanted.

Only to discover that there were still some things money couldn't buy. Respect. Acceptance. Status.

All of these were, in Connie's skewed value system, denied to her by birth. And so she turned her ambition to presenting the appearance of having them, one way or another.

It was the reason for the O'Reillys' move to Newport. It was the reason Scarlett was enrolled in a preppie private school with students named Kennedy, Du Pont and Shepard. It was the reason Scarlett was allowed, even encouraged, to date Covington Locke. And it was the reason Peyton had come along when they moved. She'd thought she could protect her little sister. She'd hoped her presence could, somehow, keep Scarlett from being overly influenced by things that weren't important…except in their mother's misguided aspirations. Above all, Peyton had wanted to be a good example of independence, generosity and right thinking.

Instead, in one reckless moment, with one fatal choice, she had thrown away her own plans, mortgaged her own future and lost any claim she had to setting a good example. And to top it off, she'd done the one thing she'd sworn she would never do…she'd accomplished her mother's life ambition. She was delivering Connie a son-in-law of impeccable breeding and a grandchild who would bear an honored and revered name.

"There's something I probably should tell you," she said, deciding Matt had a right to know. "It's about my mother."

He sighed. "Will you stop worrying about your mother? I deal with women like her every day. I'll handle any complaints she may have about the elopement. And once she knows about the baby, she won't care that we didn't have a big, fancy wedding."

Which only proved he'd never dealt with anyone like her mother.

But the gates of Danfair were in front of them

now, already opened, as if welcoming them home. It was a magnificent house, a pearl set in the midst of emerald lawns against a sapphire sea. Breathtaking and beautiful.

Except for the distracting line of vehicles parked in front.

"What is this?" Matt asked aloud, although he sounded merely curious and not as if he expected an answer.

Peyton could have given him one, though. Her heart sank when she spied her mother's favorite Mercedes coupé, sparkling gold in the winter sunshine, tucked between a white commercial van and a sleek gray Lincoln. She didn't need to see the excessively tasteful lettering on the side of the van to know Connie was here with Harold Faulkner, her decorator of choice. And she didn't have to see what was going on inside Matt's ancestral home to know that he was about to discover the very improper family he'd married into.

MATT WAS FURIOUS. Livid. Nearly four hours after the fact, he still felt outraged at walking into his home—*Danfair!*—and finding Connie O'Reilly and her entourage of decorating assistants wandering around like a gaggle of geese, pointing out problem spots, talking about the need to add color, texture and sophistication—*sophistication!*—to the rooms. The more he thought about it the angrier he became.

And he had to get over it.

In a matter of minutes, Peyton would come downstairs and they'd leave for the New Year's Eve party. Tonight, of all nights, it was imperative that he be able to act the part expected of him, that he be convincing in his role as a newlywed who was besotted with his wife. And he could have done it…easily, he believed…until Connie O'Reilly had interfered.

He glanced up at the open landing above, but could still see no sign of Peyton, so he took his cell phone from his pocket and dialed Miranda.

''Matt!'' She sounded animated, happy, backed up by the chatty laughter of a party crowd. ''When did you get back?''

''Around five.''

''Well, what's keeping you? Everyone—and I do mean *everyone*—is waiting for you to get here. The whole room is buzzing about your elopement. You and Peyton are the talk of the town—maybe of the whole state.''

''I'm waiting on Peyton to get ready,'' he said, feeling calmer as a result of making this connection with his sister. ''But I called you because when we arrived home, guess who was wandering around Danfair like she owned the place?''

"Your new mother-in-law?"

"How did you know?"

"She asked me if I thought redecorating the house for you and Peyton would be an appropriate wedding present."

He almost smiled, imagining *that* conversation. "And she decided to do it, anyway?"

"I didn't feel it was my place to tell her it wasn't appropriate, Matt."

"Why not? This is as much your home as mine."

"No, it isn't. Nate and I have decided to get married on Valentine's Day and I doubt I'll even be there that much between now and then. But even if I wasn't planning on moving out, Danfair is yours, Matt. It always has been."

He felt isolated suddenly, alone. "It *belongs* to all of us," he replied firmly. "Marriage doesn't change anything important, Miranda. It just brings in more family."

"Don't be naive. Marriage changes everything. It stands to reason it will change Danfair, too."

He couldn't believe she felt this way. "But what about Mom and Dad? What if they come home and some strange woman has redecorated everything?"

Miranda laughed. "That *strange* woman is your wife, Matt. Danfair is now her home, too. She needs to feel some ownership in it, so, of course, she'll want to make some changes…with or without her

mother's input. And our parents wouldn't notice—
or care—if the whole place was painted peacock
blue, inside and out.''

She was right about that. Charles and Linney
weren't interested in property or possessions. They
never had been and they certainly weren't going to
start now. As the oldest, Matt had taken care of the
estate business, held ownership in the house for almost as long as he could remember. ''No one's going to paint it peacock blue,'' he said, because it
was the only solid objection that came quickly to
mind.

''I know that. But, Matt, think about it. Danfair
has been like a big playground for a long time.
Maybe, now, is the right time to restore some of its
dignity. Make it a real home again, for a real family.''

''Connie O'Reilly won't be the one to do it.''

There was a slight pause, a rise in the level of
background party noise. ''Well, that's between you
and Peyton. Look, get your wife and get down to
the coffeehouse. Everyone is dying to hear about
this secretive courtship and spur-of-the-moment
elopement. Ainsley is congratulating herself all over
the place, saying she knew the minute she met Peyton that you'd fall for her, that yours would be a
surprising romance.'' She lowered her voice confid-

ingly. "Ainsley's planning an *introduction of possibilities* for Andrew tonight."

"She's becoming quite the little matchmaker, isn't she?"

"I think she's becoming exactly what she was meant to be. And, as matchmaking goes in the immediate family, she's three for four. I'm betting our Andy won't even know what hit him."

"I'm betting he won't even show tonight." Andy would be leery of his twin's newest claim to fame and her enthusiasm to include him in her list of successes.

"He will, too, show…if he knows what's good for him. I went to a lot of trouble putting this party together and my brothers had better be here."

Matt heard Nate's voice—too low and distant to be intelligible—and then she laughed—almost a giggle. In fact, if he hadn't known it was Miranda, he'd have said it was a giggle. Definitely.

"This sinfully handsome man has asked me to dance with him, and I can't say no. Get down here, Matt. You're missing all the fun." She clicked off then, leaving him no longer angry, but with an odd feeling of melancholy. His life had changed. Irrevocably. As had Miranda's. And Ainsley's. And, inevitably, as would Andrew's. Logically, of course, he'd known that, but on some deeper emotional level he'd clung to the belief that somehow, he and his siblings would always have pretty much the same life they'd always had…living at Danfair together, adding spouses and children to their odd little family, simply expanding, never really changing.

He didn't understand why he had needed that constant, but now that he saw it as the illusion it obviously was, he felt as if he'd lost his anchor, as if he'd been set adrift on a windless sea.

He heard a noise. No more than a breath of sound. Then the click of heels on the marble floor above. The whisper of fabric swaying against skin. A soft sigh of movement. Matt pulled himself together, looked up and caught his breath as a scintillating desire flashed through him like fire through dry kindling.

Peyton moved down the stairs like a dream, her hand drifting on the wide sweep of the banister railing, her head up, crowned with a halo of dark, rich curls that glistened like onyx beneath the light of the crystal chandelier. Diamonds dangled from her earlobes and gleamed like drops of dew in the hollow of her throat. Light winked and blinked with every step, caught and reflected by the sequined fabric of her deep blue gown. Even the cloak she carried draped over one arm shifted colors, shimmering from iridescent green to blue to purple and an occasional glimmer of red. From head to foot, she sparkled like the promise of the new year. Her hazel eyes had picked up a blue cast from the dress, and her lips were tinted a luscious rose.

There was no hint of a smile, though. Merely a paleness in her cheeks and a stalwart lift to her chin. As if she were about to go into battle rather than out to a party.

As she reached the base of the staircase, a wave of pride and protectiveness washed over him, grounding him in his new role as husband and father. Peyton needed him. He had promised to keep his end of their bargain and for the duration of their marriage, he would stand between her and the rest of the world. No one would ever know from his actions that this wasn't exactly what it appeared to be—a love match.

Moving forward, he offered her his hand for the last step. She looked at it for a moment, as if undecided, then laid her fingers in his palm. Her skin felt cold and he closed the warmth of his hand around hers. "Nice outfit," he said.

"Thank you." Her voice was barely more than a breath. "I bought it on our shopping trip, remember? So I'd have something suitable for tonight."

"I remember sitting in a little pink chair, waiting while you tried on dresses." He remembered trying to blend into the scenery, feeling uncomfortable among the feminine finery and the women who were there to either buy or sell it. He remembered how small the chair had felt and he remembered wondering what women did that took so long. He did not, however, remember this dress. Nor could he ever have imagined how completely breathtaking she would look in it. "Now," he offered as an apology for having forgotten, "I realize it was more than worth the wait."

A ghost of a smile floated across her lips and vanished as quickly as it had appeared. "I'm really sorry about this afternoon," she said quickly, as if she'd been practicing the words for some time. "I know you were angry. And you have every right to be. Mother shouldn't have talked her way into the house. Or brought that annoying Charles with her. I'll take care of it, Matt. Don't worry. She's not going to do anything to this house. I promise."

His melancholy bloomed into desire and all he could think about was how much he wanted to pull her into his arms and kiss her. He gazed at the curve of her lips, fascinated by the way she moistened them with the tip of her tongue, mesmerized by the scent of her perfume. "Decorating the house for us is a nice thought, a generous gift," he said magnanimously, because there was no reason to be angry with her for the overbearing ways of her mother. "But you should be the one to make those decisions, Peyton. Not your mother."

Her gaze flew to his, confused, questioning. "I

wouldn't dream of changing your home," she said. "It...well, I just wouldn't."

"Why not? The place—" he paused, recalling Miranda's words, realizing she was right "—could use a little dignity. It's been a showroom, a playground for too long. I think I'd like it to be a home again. A place you'll feel comfortable living."

"I won't be here long enough to become comfortable, Matt." The change in her voice, the defensive lift of her chin mimicked the chill in her touch, bringing him up short against reality. "There is no reason for you to change anything on my account."

And that was about as plainly as she could put it. This was a marriage of convenience, a way to put a positive spin on their mistake, a lie to protect the baby they had accidentally created. He withdrew his hand, letting hers drop to her side. "The car's out front," he said briskly. "Are you ready to face the lions?"

"Ready," she replied firmly and stepped ahead of him toward the door.

Not the way he'd pictured the beginning of their charade. But he'd be damned if he was going to let her goad him into giving away the show before the curtain even went up. He'd been playing one role or another since birth. This was simply one more to add to his repertoire.

The anger returned as suddenly as it had receded,

but this time it was controlled and purposeful. Following her out into the crisp, cold night, he arrived on the stoop in time to help her put on the cloak. It had a hood, which settled in folds around her neck, rippling out toward her shoulders, framing her face in its flickering colors and yet taking nothing at all away from her own beauty. Her eyes, still mystifyingly hazel beneath the stars and the outside lighting, met his, clung for a moment. A heartbeat thudded loudly—his, he supposed—in the seconds before he raised his palms and framed her face.

"Happy New Year, Mrs. Danville." He lowered his head swiftly, deliberately, and didn't stop even when he felt her stiffen with resistance. His lips claimed hers with a rough insistence, refused to let her deny them both the pleasure of this provocative kiss. She held out for a moment, but then, with a quivery sigh, her hands came up to rest on his arms; her fingers pulsed and massaged his biceps, letting him know her yearning was as intense, as irrefutable as his own. Marriage hadn't changed that, he realized. The passion flared as quickly between them now as it had before, growing dangerously willful, treacherously unyielding. It burned him as well as her, singeing his control, melting her resistance. She relaxed against him, her breasts pressed invitingly to his chest, her lips opened. He took advantage and delivered hot, sipping kisses until her tongue ventured out to meet his in a seductive tryst. His self-restraint—what little he seemed to possess with this woman—ebbed faster than sand in an hourglass and he knew he was within minutes—seconds—of sweeping her up in his arms and carrying her back inside the house.

And he was almost positive she wouldn't murmur a single protest. It was what she wanted, too. He knew it the same way he knew he couldn't allow that to happen. For more reasons than he cared to contemplate. Yet, when she moaned softly, sensually against his lips, he deepened the kiss and tussled with the possibility again. Logic won over desire by the smallest margin this time, and he felt as if he was forcing his ardor into a lockbox out of sheer necessity.

It was an experiment gone awry, a test of will he had obviously failed, but even so, Matt managed to marshal his defenses and drew back from the kiss, dropping his hands to her arms and establishing control by the expedient means of putting some distance between them. Emotional distance, as well as physical. "So much for practicing," he said more huskily than he meant to…because his voice, as well as his body, was still hostage to the alluring desire. But he made it seem light, unimportant, as if he hadn't been affected by the kiss at all, as if he hadn't noticed its effect on her. "I think we're ready for the main event, now, don't you?"

She blinked, but recovered her composure as she drew the cloak closed around her, somehow signifying her disapproval and, however reluctantly, her disappointment. "Ready or not, Matt, rehearsal is over. It's time to face the music."

Chapter Six

"Your brother looks happy." Ivan slipped his arm around Ainsley and drew her lovingly against his side.

"Mmm." She nestled into him, while observing Matt with a meditative eye. "Which one?"

"Matt, obviously," Ivan said. "Since Andrew doesn't look happy at all."

She couldn't quite suppress her giggle. "He looks perfectly miserable, doesn't he? I imagine Rachel is telling him, at length, about her trip to Africa. She loves to talk about it, and he can't get away because of his broken ankle." Ainsley gave a deep and highly dramatic sigh. "You know it's difficult even for a matchmaker to predict just how an introduction of possibilities will go."

Ivan kissed the top of her head. "Then why do I get the feeling you're not at all unhappy about how this particular one is turning out?"

"Maybe because it's turning out exactly as I hoped it would. With someone as wily as my twin, a matchmaker has to be very careful not to tip her hand."

"Ah-ha," Ivan said knowingly. "So your strategy is to mislead your prey...er, I mean, client, not to mention get someone to bore him to tears, and all the while you're planning to sneak up and shove him off a cliff in the opposite direction."

She looked up at him, adoring this man who was her husband and best friend. "You're getting good at this, Doctor," she said. "You wouldn't be angling for an apprentice position at IF Enterprises, would you?"

"Oh, no," he declared firmly. "I have my hands full with the pediatric center."

"Well, it's a good thing. You'd probably be better than I am and I wouldn't like that at all."

"No one could be better than you, Ainsley."

She loved him for that...because he believed it...and for a million other reasons. "I want my brothers to be as happy in love as we are, Ivan, as happy as Miranda and Nate are going to be."

"It certainly appears you've been successful with Matt. Look at the way he's holding Peyton...as if she were made of spun glass."

Ainsley thought it looked more as if he were holding something he was terrified of breaking. Which was not the same thing at all. Not to her match-maker's eye. Peyton was the right woman for her brother. Ainsley had no doubts about that, but their sudden elopement after all these months of pretending they couldn't be in the same room without an argument… Well, something didn't seem quite right about that. She just didn't know what it was.

The music changed and Peyton and Matt separated. She danced off with Nate, he with Miranda. Ainsley considered the nagging feeling that this perfect match didn't quite live up to its romantic hype. Even if Matt did look happier than he had in a long time.

"Would you care to dance, Mrs. Donovan?" Ivan bent his head to whisper seductively into her ear.

And her knees went weak with longing—a regular occurrence in her marriage. She went up on tiptoe to kiss him full on the lips.

"I should ask you to dance more often," he said when the kiss ended.

She smiled, so in love she sometimes couldn't see straight. "I would love to dance with you," she said. "But you'll have to hold that thought for a few minutes. There's something I need to do first. I think Andrew has suffered enough and is overdue for a rescue. Plus, if I read the signs correctly—and I'm sure I do—Rachel's true match is getting miffed. *Just* as I planned."

"Who is he?" he asked, turning around to see if he could spot Rachel's *true* match by his disgruntled expression. But no young man anywhere close by seemed to fit the description. "Anyone I know?"

She smiled and patted his cheek. "I have to keep some secrets, even from you, Ivan. Can't risk information getting out accidentally before its time. Save that dance for me. I'll be back in a flash. Or two. Three at the most." With a grin that crinkled her nose and brought out her dimples, she sighed dramatically. "A matchmaker's work is never done, you know."

Then she whisked off, to bring the new-and-improved Hayley Sayers out of hiding.

Unless she missed her guess—and she was ninety-nine point nine percent certain that she hadn't—Andrew would never know Cupid had a dead aim on his heart.

"So, HOW LONG have you been dating my sister?"

Scarlett O'Reilly wore a dress that was too mature for her and that merely emphasized the innocence she so unknowingly projected. Her hair was long and dark like Peyton's, but her eyes were a vivid, vibrant green and—in Matt's opinion—already somewhat jaded. She was a pretty young woman, trying too hard to appear more grown-up than she actually was. Peyton was right to be concerned about her. "Several months," he answered her question. "Since she began volunteering at the Foundation office."

Scarlett eyed him suspiciously. "Why'd you keep it such a secret? Were you ashamed to be seen with her?"

"Of course not." Where had this child—she was, after all, only fifteen—picked up such a defensive attitude? "We're private people." He repeated the explanation he'd been offering, in one form or another, all evening. "We'd found something very special…and we simply didn't want to share it."

Obviously unconvinced, Scarlett sipped a drink that Matt strongly suspected held more alcohol than his own. "Well, I think the whole deal sounds a little too much like a fairy tale."

"There are such things as happy endings, Scarlett."

"There's also such a thing as a good beginning, and eloping is a shady way to do anything so important. Mom is plenty mad about it, too. She's been planning mine and Peyton's weddings for years."

He'd successfully avoided his maddening mother-in-law so far tonight, and he wasn't about to get into a discussion about her with her teenage daughter. "Getting married is very personal, Scarlett. Your sister and I did it the way we wanted, which is our prerogative."

Scarlett's green-eyed glare nailed him in place. "You'd better make her happy, Matt. Or it'll be my prerogative to make sure you regret it."

Her threat was so surprising, he almost laughed, but there was a steely determination in her tone, and his evolving opinion of her shifted slightly. He admired her spunk in challenging him, and he respected her because she cared about her sister's happiness. Matt decided to give her the benefit of the doubt. "I believe you might try," he said with his best hey-we're-on-the-same-team-here smile.

"I'm a lot tougher than Peyton, you know."

"I happen to think she's plenty tough. She can argue me to a standstill—and that's not easy."

"Arguing is her way of keeping anyone from suspecting she's not as tough as she pretends to be. I mean it, Matt. Be careful with her."

Not so much a threat now as a warning. Surprising, too, in its focus and maturity. But unnecessary, as he felt he was being extremely careful with Peyton. Witness the number of times he'd rescued her just this evening from too-curious guests who were pressing for the details of their romance. He'd taken over the lies, lessened the strain on her and soothed a good deal of rampant inquisitiveness at the same time. He'd played his role convincingly and with a confident smile...the same way he'd played every other role in his life. Inside, he might be a bundle of twitching nerves, but on the outside, he was exactly the happy bridegroom he appeared to be.

And if the script demanded that he charm Scarlett into believing his and Peyton's was a fairy-tale romance, then that's exactly what he would do. Setting his glass aside, he reached for hers. "I'm always very careful, Scarlett. And now that we understand each other, would you like to dance with your new brother-in-law?"

She debated momentarily, looking doubtfully from her glass to him, but finally she allowed him to take it from her.

Round one to him, he thought as he set the glass aside and led her onto the dance floor.

PEYTON WATCHED Matt dancing with Scarlett and thought how handsome he was. It almost hurt her heart to look at him. He had a great smile, warm and appealing, and he was clearly charming the socks off her little sister, which was no small accomplishment in itself. He whirled Scarlett around the floor, making her laugh, and proving that he was a wonderful dancer, too. Something Peyton had never felt particularly competent at. But then, Matt had been born to dance in gilded ballrooms in a tuxedo made exclusively for him, while she still felt like an impostor, all dressed up in her mother's clothes like a child trying to catch a glimpse of herself as a grown-up.

"Congratulations, Peyton," Connie said, walking up beside her. "I didn't think you had it in you."

"Had what?"

"The wiles to get the most eligible bachelor in Newport to marry you."

Peyton pressed her lips together in a tight frown and reminded herself that in Connie's view, denial usually equated to guilt. "You're supposed to congratulate the groom, Mother," she replied calmly but with effort. "Not the bride. And I'm still very angry with you about this afternoon. Matt didn't like your being there, either."

Connie smiled. "He'll get over it, darling, and so will you. I'm giving you a very generous wedding present and I'm not about to apologize for it. Especially not now that I've seen the inside of that house. Frankly, Danfair is a mess."

"I like it just the way it is. And, more important, so does Matt. It's his home and I'm not going to start out our marriage by changing things."

"Of course you are, sweetie. That's what wives do. We change things. We make them better. Trust me. Husbands appreciate their wives taking the responsibility of creating an attractive environment for them to come home to."

"No, Mother. Thank you for the thought, but I

don't want the house redecorated as a wedding gift.''

"You'll change your mind when all that clutter begins to drive you insane," Connie said with certainty. "But perhaps it was a bit precipitate for me to have been there when you arrived."

"Being there, with those…people…when we returned from our honeymoon was just plain *pushy*."

"It was simply expedient, darling. Those *people* are very busy, very much in demand. They charge a fortune, you know, because they're the best and they made a special effort for me by going to Danfair this afternoon. You should be grateful."

The story of her life. "Don't do anything like that again, Mother. I don't appreciate it and I guarantee you that Matt didn't like it one little bit."

Connie sipped her drink, unperturbed. "He didn't act as if it bothered him at all."

"He was being polite. For my sake. We did just get married, you know."

"Yes, you did, didn't you?" Connie smiled—her favorite cat-who-caught-the-canary smile. "And I'm excessively proud of you for it, too, although I must say that this elopement came as something of a shock to me. Getting Matt's thoughtful note was a surprise, to say the least. I will confess I hoped you'd take a little bit of initiative once we settled in Newport and you became acquainted with a few suitable men, but I never in my wildest dreams suspected you had it in you to land such a big fish.''

Peyton closed her eyes, took a deep breath and tried wishing away the unsettled churning in her stomach. "He isn't a *fish,* and I didn't *land* him. He's a wonderful man and I married him."

"Which I find ironic, considering how many times in the past year you've told me you planned to marry the poorest redneck you could find simply to aggravate me. I never actually believed you meant it, of course, although I'll confess I didn't believe you'd ever, in a million years, choose a man I couldn't find a single fault with."

"Keep looking, Mother. I'm sure you'll find one."

"Are you kidding?" Connie said with a laugh. "Honey, the Danville name is on every who's who list in America, every social register in New England, and the whole family are members of a very elite class who can trace their ancestry clear back to the first colonists. Their fortune is staggering. Matthew inherits Danfair and heads up a highly revered foundation worth billions of dollars. I get goose bumps thinking that *my* grandson will be the first in his generation and the first in line to inherit all that."

Peyton's stomach made a painful flop. "You're being pushy again, Mother."

Turning, Connie lifted her eyebrows. "Oh, please,

Peyton. I'm not completely unaware of what goes on in your life. For the past couple of months, you've been pale and quiet, your appetite has been either nonexistent or completely out of control. I know you've been sick. I can see the change in your body already. You're pregnant. Pretend all you want with everyone else, but I'm your mother and I know why Matthew Danville married you.''

And despite herself, Peyton felt a sense of relief. Keeping the secret had made her edgy and nervous, sharing it with Matt had merely amplified her sense of panic. She'd wished she could talk to her mother so many times since she'd suspected and then confirmed the pregnancy, even though she'd realized that Connie would be no help at all.

Connie had hated being pregnant with Scarlett. Peyton well remembered all the complaints during those months, how her mother had resented the time she'd had to be away from the restaurant, how she'd blamed Rick for the accidental pregnancy, how he'd laughed at her charge, refusing to believe she wasn't as delighted as he. Before that time, Peyton hadn't even suspected she'd been an accident, too. But Connie had made it clear she'd never intended to have children, never would have had even one child if she'd thought Rick would marry her otherwise. But she'd had two daughters, and discovered—much to her own surprise—that instead of interfering with her ambition, they could be her winning lottery tickets for the status and acceptance she'd always craved.

Peyton hated the fact that she was giving Connie what she wanted, and yet felt a sickening, abysmal pride at having, at last, done something that pleased her mother. "I love Matt," she said, and for a moment it felt like the truth. "That's why I married him. Please don't turn this into some lurid sacrifice I made for your sake."

Connie laughed. "You'd be a fool not to love him, dear. He's absolutely perfect. You're the envy of every single woman—and several married ones—here tonight, including me. He's everything I've ever wanted for you."

He was everything she'd ever wanted for herself. Her daughters were simply a means to an end. "I didn't marry Matt for you," she replied succinctly.

"Oh, I know you didn't, sweetie. You did it for the baby…and Matt did it because he can't afford the scandal of having fathered an illegitimate child. In his position, he has to be careful about what others think." Raising the glass, Connie tipped it in a silent toast. "I don't care why or how you trapped him into this marriage, Peyton. But don't mess this up. The Danville connections will give Scarlett all the social advantages your father and I can't. This is going to be great for her."

"And it won't do you any harm either, will it?" Peyton snipped off the words, angry with her mother, Matt, everyone. She wasn't a calculating manipulator like Connie. She hadn't set out to get pregnant. She hadn't trapped Matt into this marriage. She'd never wanted to give Scarlett anything more than the chance to form her own values and make her own choices.

"I've never been shy about saying what I want, Peyton. You've done a wonderful thing for all of us…providing, of course, that Matt is actually the father of that baby." She held up a hand. "*Don't.* I know you're outraged by the idea, but it's a question that will come up, Peyton. People being what they are. You may as well get ready for it."

She was too angry, too upset to speak, but Connie had no problem filling in the gap with an even more offensive observation. "And, honestly, I doubt it matters, because if he married you to avoid the scandal of illegitimacy, then he'll do *anything* to avoid admitting you hoodwinked him into claiming a child that isn't even his."

The anger boiled over then, spilling hot and acidic through Peyton's veins. Her stomach roiled from the stress, and the sickness came in a wave. She couldn't fight it down, hard as she tried and, spinning on her heel, Peyton raced to the ladies' room.

"I SEEM to have lost track of my wife," Matt said.

"Happens to me all the time," Ivan responded. "Ainsley's right here one minute, spinning away like a yo-yo without a string the next. I'm just happy she always comes back to me." He clapped Matt on the shoulder. "Don't worry. Peyton's around here somewhere. She may even be in on the rescue."

Matt raised his eyebrows in question. "What rescue?"

"Ainsley has a plan to rescue Andy. It's some sort of big surprise."

"With Ainsley, everything is a big surprise."

"You're one to talk," Ivan said. "You managed a major surprise this week, yourself. Even Ainsley didn't expect an elopement."

"That was the idea. We wanted a quiet wedding and we'd never have had it if we'd told anyone we were getting married. You know how my sisters are. They'd have been in the big middle of planning a wedding extravaganza before the words were out of my mouth."

"Good point. Plus, there's no telling what your new mother-in-law would have planned."

"She wants to redecorate the house as a wedding present."

"Danfair? You're kidding."

Matt shook his head, still scanning the crowd for a glimpse of Peyton's dark hair and the shimmer of her blue gown. "I came close to tossing my new mother-in-law out the door this afternoon."

"You mean she was *there* when you got home?"

"With a crew of designers. Luckily, Peyton got to her before I did and convinced her they needed to leave. It was all I could do to remain civil."

This time, Ivan was left shaking his head. "I don't know how that pushy woman ever managed to produce a sweetheart like Peyton. Ainsley is crazy about her and, I'll confess that if I wasn't so full-moon loco about my wife, I might have a bit of a crush on her, myself. She's definitely worth the aggravation of putting up with a less-than-desirable set of in-laws, don't you agree? Well, of course you do." Ivan grinned. "You married her, after all."

"Yes," Matt said. "I did." His gaze skirted the dance floor, searching for a glimpse of blue. Instead, he saw Connie watching him from across the room and, when she caught his eye, she lifted her glass in a salute. He passed right over her, as if he hadn't noticed, saw Miranda and Nate, his cousin Scott, and his wife, Molly. He saw Bryce and Lara Braddock talking with Bryce's father, James and his wife, Ilsa…who was actually responsible for all this matchmaking nonsense, but who was such a lovely lady it was hard to find any fault in her. He saw Andrew reaching for his crutches, and George Millston's daughter—Matt couldn't remember her name at the moment—trying to help. Andy didn't look as if he needed help and Matt was certain he didn't want any. But—*Rachel! That* was her name— looked determined to help him nonetheless. Matt continued his search for Peyton, but still didn't see her anywhere and felt a prick of concern.

"Wow!" Ivan muttered beside him. "Would you look at that?"

That was the young woman standing with Ainsley by the entrance. Of course, knowing how crazy in love Ivan was, his *wow* could have been meant for his wife. But it was the woman with her who actually deserved the attention. Hayley Sayers looked like a movie star—one of the current crop of incredibly cute ones—with her red hair razored into a sassy style, her moss-green gown dipping low enough to reveal that she did, indeed, have breasts, the fabric clinging just tightly enough to show off the rest of her slender but impressive shape—a fact that would have been hard to guess from her usual attire. Matt had seen her only a couple of times in the several months since she'd gone to work as Andy's assistant. But her customary baggy jeans, T-shirt, no makeup and truly awful hairstyle hadn't offered a hint that she could look like this. And the way Andrew talked about her, Matt had thought his brother viewed her as an assistant with potential, but little more than background, a shadow when he needed one in a picture, someone to help tote his equipment or hold his camera while he sought the best angle for a shot.

But whatever Andy's true feelings, everything was about to change.

Courtesy of Ainsley, their own personal matchmaker. She wouldn't be happy until all her siblings were married, no matter what their own desire might be in the matter. Getting Andrew to recognize an *introduction of possibilities* was the reason for Hayley's dramatic transformation. Ainsley had helped create the same kind of stunning makeover with Peter Braddock's wife, Thea. Except this metamorphosis proved more startling by far.

Matt glanced over at Andrew, who had made his escape from Rachel and didn't yet realize he was a bull's-eye and was only seconds away from being struck with the dart of possibilities. The Apprentice Matchmaker does it again, Matt thought, feeling a little sorry for his younger brother. The poor guy didn't stand a chance.

"Isn't she something?" Ivan's voice was thick with pride and, this time, there could be no question who he meant.

"Yes," Matt agreed. "Your little matchmaker is really something. I don't think I can stand here and watch Andrew get blindsided, though. I'm going to look for Peyton."

He circled the dance floor and had just reached the other side, when the deejay announced, "Folks, it's almost that magic hour. Get your noisemakers ready and your lips puckered. The new year is only minutes away."

"And you still owe me a dance from this year."

A light touch on his arm stopped him and Matt turned to look down at Jessica, who laughingly tugged him toward the dance floor.

"I'll have to give you a rain check," he said.

"That's what you said the last time I asked you to dance. The least you can do is make good on *that* rain check before you go offering me another one. Come on, Matthew. You know you want to."

He didn't, but he knew she wouldn't let it drop. She wanted what she wanted and she didn't give up without a fight, however genteel her tactics. So he gave in gracefully and danced with her. "You look lovely tonight, as always, Jessica. Where's Jon?"

"He's here somewhere," she answered with a pretty shrug. "Probably flirting like mad with someone. Already over the legal limit."

"On flirting or alcohol?"

She smiled up at him in a way he knew would beguile most men.

"Both, I imagine. My husband is quite the charmer when he's drunk. Unfortunately, I didn't realize until after the wedding that I'd never seen him sober.'' She edged closer, her body curving suggestively into his as they made a turn. ''I can't talk about this…problem…with just anyone, Matthew, and I don't know what I'd have done this past year if you hadn't been there to listen. I hope Peyton will understand that you and I have a special sort of friendship.''

Under the cover of an extra dance step, he reestablished a respectful distance between his body and hers. He'd actually never considered Jessica a particular friend. She was a co-worker and, by the very nature of their positions, they spent a great deal of time together…much of it social. She had hinted at her husband's drinking problem, but nothing she'd told him was a big secret. Everyone knew about Jon's excesses, and Matt had always been careful to maintain a proper distance in his relationship with Jessica. Mostly because he suspected she wanted more than his friendship and he couldn't afford any hint of scandal. Even groundless gossip about him having an affair with a married woman could have a negative effect on contributions and the Foundation's mission. ''Don't give it another thought,'' he said. ''Peyton knows she has no reason to feel threatened by my relationship with anyone else. She's not the jealous type.''

''Oh, well, of course not,'' Jessica amended. ''I didn't mean to suggest she was. I just thought, since she and I have often been at odds, she might say something that would…affect your opinion of me.''

''I can't see that happening, Jessica.''

The beguiling smile returned. ''Good. I won't worry about it then, and you and I will simply go on as we always have. Marriage doesn't really change anything, after all.''

But she was wrong. Matt could see the truth in that. He felt the difference in himself already. He didn't just think he *ought* to dance with Peyton, he actually *wanted* to dance with her, wanted to be where she was. No other woman held any interest for him. The feeling surprised him, but it felt pleasant, too. It was almost a new year, almost a new beginning, and he wanted to start it with his wife. *Wife.* What an extraordinary concept. ''Sorry to cut this short, Jessica, but I'd like to find Peyton before—''

''Okay, folks, here we go. Ten…nine…eight…'' The deejay started counting down the seconds and the crowd picked up the chant.

The music stopped to accommodate the excitement and Matt stepped away from Jessica to look for Peyton in the crowd…on the edges…near the doors. Where in hell was she?

''…three…two…one… Happy New Year!'' Noisemakers, whistles, laughter and dozens yelling, ''Happy New Year!'' all hit the airwaves at the same moment, and Matt, distracted by his search, was surprised to find himself abruptly pulled into a kiss. A seductive, wanton and very determined kiss. He broke it off immediately, setting Jessica away from him and turning a deaf ear to her "Happy New Year, Matthew."

He pushed through the merrymakers surrounding them, concerned about Peyton, certain that someone had noted the kiss, certain that Jessica had meant for it to be seen, and very much aware that it was Peyton he wanted to kiss.

PEYTON HAD SEEN THE KISS. Just as she'd left the ladies' room, she'd heard the horns, whistles and a chorus of "Happy New Year!" "Auld Lang Syne" came blasting over the speakers, surrounding her in the nostalgia that came with the end of one year and the beginning of another. And then there, directly in her line of vision, was her husband kissing another woman.

No, not just another woman. Jessica.

Jealousy tore through her already shaky composure. She wanted to stride onto the dance floor and jerk him away, scream at him for being an idiot, humiliate him…hurt him. As seeing that kiss had hurt her. But making a scene would spoil the illusion they'd both—supposedly—worked all evening to convey. Not that kissing Jessica would do anything to promote the idea that Matt was completely devoted to his wife, but if Peyton behaved like a shrew, it would only make everything worse. She'd give vent to her frustration another time, but for now, she'd just have to pretend she felt so secure in his love, the sight of him kissing someone else was not a threat.

Then, in case she might have missed seeing it, Scarlett was quickly beside her to report. "Matt kissed that woman," she said. "Why did you let him do that?"

"I was in the ladies' room," she replied tersely.

"Oh, so as long as you're out of the room, he can kiss anyone he wants?"

"It's New Year's Eve, Scarlett, and people kiss perfect strangers at midnight. It doesn't mean anything."

"She's not a perfect stranger and it means something. You should give him hell."

Peyton agreed. Totally. And it galled her to be put in a position of having to defend him. Especially after the performance they'd put on all evening. But at least she owed Jessica no allegiance whatsoever. "You're right," she said tightly. "Jessica isn't a stranger. She's an opportunist, and there's nothing she would enjoy more than to embarrass me tonight. I refuse to give her that satisfaction. Now, this discussion is over."

"You mean you don't care?"

"Scarlett," she said on a sigh, "I don't want to talk about this."

"So you're not jealous that your husband kissed a woman you detest?"

"I'm *not* jealous."

"I don't understand you, Peyton. You should be out there giving him a good hard kick in the—"

"Found you at last. I was beginning to think you'd left without me." Matt's voice came from behind her, caressed her with its husky tone, soothed her inner turmoil so easily it should have made her even angrier.

But instead, the heat of her anger transformed with a sizzle into ravenous desire. She wanted him, suddenly and forcefully. She wanted hot, breathless kisses and hungry hands on her body. She wanted to writhe naked beneath him, taste him with long, sweet licks of her tongue. The craving shivered inside her like a dark cloud, stirring warm winds and cold air to create a storm. Great. Just what she needed to make this horrible evening complete. "No," she said firmly to the desire…but her voice came out shaky and vulnerable.

His hands, warm and strong, took her arms and turned her around. His smile could have melted a polar ice cap…which she wasn't. Not by a long shot. Oh, no, she was on fire. Burning with the reckless attraction that had taken over her body and made her putty in his hands. Okay, so she wasn't putty, either. More like molten lava. "Where were you?" he asked. "I was looking everywhere for you."

"Hmmph," Scarlett snorted, her voice low enough to carry only as far as Peyton's ears. "He must have thought you were down Jessica's throat."

"Scarlett," Peyton warned.

"Well, it's true!" Scarlett flounced away, as offended and furious as Peyton wanted to be.

His glance followed her for an instant. "What's wrong with her?" he asked.

Peyton sighed. Pretending took a lot out of a person. Especially a pregnant person. "She's fifteen," she said, falling back on the old airtight excuse.

"Then let's not waste time talking about her. Not now that I've finally got you where I want you." Smiling lazily, he pulled her into his arms as if he had nothing to apologize for, and tipped up her chin with one finger. "Happy New Year, wife." He bent his head and kissed her soundly, thoroughly, tenderly, taking his time and letting the kiss linger in its own pleasure. The noise around them faded into the background, unintrusive and unimportant. The crowd melted from her consciousness. Matt was the only thing left in that heartbeat of a moment. His lips on hers the only reality, the heat of his body all the invitation her body required. She ached for his touch. Her heart cried out for tenderness, a show of respectful care. It had been a tense and stressful evening. She'd take whatever comfort she could find in him, even if he was only pretending. She let go of caring that he'd kissed Jessica. For the moment, she couldn't care less if he'd kissed every other woman in the room before he came to her. She only cared that he was kissing her now. And that he kept on kissing her until she no longer cared if she could breathe.

But he pulled back, in what she chose to interpret as a fog of reluctance, and she was left feeling weak and clingy, staring up at him, bewitched and bewildered. "Can we get out of here now?" she whispered.

He stroked her cheek with the back of his hand, kissed her again. Lightly. Sweetly. "That's the best idea I've heard this year. Let's go."

She would have gone with him anywhere.

But she was grateful they were simply going home.

Chapter Seven

Matt tossed his keys on a table in the foyer and began looking through a stack of mail on the credenza. "Andrew is staying at the beach house for the time being," he explained matter-of-factly. "He said he didn't want to intrude on the newlyweds."

Peyton slipped off her cloak, stood holding it self-consciously, not sure if there was a coat closet nearby or if she was expected to keep it with her in her room. The staff at Danfair wasn't expected to be front and center every time a family member returned home, as Connie insisted on in the O'Reilly household. The only Danville employee Peyton had met so far was a young man from Guatemala, whose main job, it appeared, was learning English. Matt had introduced him as Frederico, asked him a question in Spanish, and then complimented him on his halting, almost incomprehensible English answer.

There was no pretense in this house, no effort to

showcase the family's wealth with designer rooms and furnishings meant to be admired and appreciated for their expensive luster. Peyton could feel the difference here. It was a mood, as much as anything, a sense of great love and gratitude for the blessings held within these walls. Four children had grown up here, basically making and breaking their own rules. The remnants of that life were still strewn about— the toys and games, the croquet set. Her mother was right about one thing. Danfair was a mess. A mess composed of memories and laughter and a close-knit, loving family. A mess made by four children who somehow managed to spin their straw into gold. And, for Peyton, that's what made the difference. That's what made it a home.

"Miranda's staying with the Shepards this week," Matt continued. "Nate's mother is home from Florida for the holidays and they have family activities planned for tomorrow."

Was he pointing out to her—in a decidedly off-hand manner—that they were alone in the house tonight? Was he indicating, perhaps, he didn't want to sleep alone, in their adjoining, but separate, bedrooms? A quiver of possibilities skittered all the way from her head to her toes. She hesitated, nervous energy making her restless, uncertain. "Miranda's inherited quite a family. I can't imagine having one set of twins, much less two."

He set aside a magazine, one of many in the mail that had accumulated during their week away from Newport, and answered only absently. "And one set are thirteen, going on thirty."

"Thirteen is a difficult age."

"Yes," Matt agreed, although she doubted he even knew what she'd said.

Then again, she wasn't really saying anything. Just filling an awkward moment with empty conversation.

"We're invited." He began sifting larger envelopes into one pile, smaller into another. "If you want to go."

"Where?"

"To the Shepards. Tomorrow."

"What for?"

He glanced at her, as if she hadn't been paying attention. "It's New Year's Day, Peyton. Families get together. Eat dinner. Watch football." His expression changed suddenly, became politely wary. "You, uh, weren't planning for us to spend the holiday tomorrow with your family, were you?"

"No," she said quickly, wanting that even less than he did. After tonight, she'd really rather not see anyone for several days. But she definitely wasn't going anywhere near her mother. "No. We can spend the day with Nate and Miranda, if you'd like."

He went back to sorting the mail into separate stacks. "I think that ought to be your decision, Peyton."

"Then I'd prefer to stay here."

He nodded, giving no indication if he'd have preferred to go or stay.

"You can go without me," she suggested, knowing she'd hate it if he did. "I don't mind."

The corners of his lips tipped up in a slight smile as he singled out one envelope to open. "That would look a little odd, considering we haven't even been married a whole week yet."

It struck her that her married life was going to be a repeat of her years of living with her mother—where every choice was based on how it might appear to someone else. "We can go, if you'd rather," she offered.

"I'd rather not," he said absently, reading the letter he'd pulled out of the envelope. "Tonight was more than enough socializing for me. I thought midnight would never come."

She had felt the same, and yet, hearing him voice relief that their first appearance as a couple was over stirred her own dissatisfaction. "I'm going to bed," she said firmly, frustrated by his lack of attention and her need for it. She wanted kisses, fevered caresses, mindless, melting passion. She wanted to exhaust her restlessness in his bed, find a release for her pent up emotions, and…yes…punish him for kissing Jessica. Which she suddenly realized bothered her more than it should. More even than her mother's awful comments. If he offered even a minimum of encouragement, she would show him she was twice the woman Jessica was. Ten times. A hundred times.

"I'm going to bed," she repeated.

He didn't even glance up at her over the top of the stupid letter. "Good night, then."

Obviously, he had no thought of sweeping her off her feet and carrying her up the stairs to bed. He hadn't carried her over the threshold, either. At Danfair or at the Niagara Falls house. Which might be expecting a little too much from a temporary husband, she supposed. But she couldn't keep from sighing, long and deeply, as she marched past him. And she couldn't help letting the cloak swish against the backs of his pant legs with a seductive whisper…or allowing it to droop behind her in a sifting kaleidoscope of color when he didn't seem to notice.

"Peyton?"

Halfway up the stairs, she turned, her hand on the curved banister, the cloak draping around her feet in an iridescent pool, hating herself for feeling so hopeful, so desperately needy. "Yes?"

"Good job tonight. I think we pulled it off."

The words, the tone, the message were all wrong.

It felt too much like an afterthought, a pat on the head from a condescending uncle. "Do you really, Matt?" she asked coolly.

His eyebrows rose at the sarcasm in her voice. "Well, I did until just this minute."

The anger was back suddenly. Bathed in disappointment. Colored with frustration. Tainted by the desire she couldn't seem to banish. But anger, nonetheless. "Well, I think actions speak louder than words."

His forehead furrowed, as if he was replaying the evening, looking for anything he might have missed. "Are you saying my actions left something to be desired?"

He had a lot of nerve to sound so offended. "Hmm, let me think," she said, deliberately baiting him. "Yes, as a matter of fact, I believe they did. I believe they left a *lot* to be desired."

"Meaning what?"

How could he pretend he didn't know to what she was referring? But then, he was very good at pretending. Witness how warm and caring he'd been in front of an audience, how cool and quiet in the car coming home. "Meaning I saw you and Jessica."

"Jessica?" His tone was all confused innocence, as if he didn't—*couldn't*—remember. "Dancing?"

"A little more than that. You kissed her."

"I did not. She kissed me."

Peyton swished the cloak until it made a silky hiss of disagreement. "Well, that explains it."

"Explains what?" Irritation rumbled in his voice, warned her.

"Oh, that's good, Matthew. I believe you are getting this marriage act down pat. Why, that sounded just like a husband, falsely accused and having to defend his exemplary actions."

He moved toward her like a thundercloud, then abruptly stopped three stair steps below her. Her heart was in her throat, her pulse racing as she waited, watching while he stroked his jaw and the muscle clenching there. "I can't believe you're bringing this up now."

She lifted her shoulder in a shrug she knew he'd find annoying. "Now seems as good a time as any. Unless you'd rather explain yourself to my sister."

"I have no intention of explaining anything I do to Scarlett. What does she have to do with this, anyway?"

His anger was rising. Peyton could feel the heat of it, the intensity of his battle to keep from losing patience with her. They'd been in this position before. Many times. But it had always centered around the Foundation, the way he let Jessica run roughshod over the staff, while sweet-talking her way around the volunteers. It hadn't been so…personal. Exhilarating, yes. Exciting, too. Flirting with the attraction, masking it with argument, skirting passion with agitation. But never before so intensely personal. And Peyton, rashly, gave it another push. "Scarlett saw you kiss Jessica," she said. "And she is sorely disappointed in you."

"Disappointed!" His hand ransacked his hair. The muscle in his jaw snapped taut. Then he was beside her, his eyes blazing with a week's worth of aggravation. "I didn't *do* anything. If you'd had the sense to act like the besotted wife you're supposed to be, you'd have told your sister that even if I had kissed someone else—which I didn't—it meant nothing. Absolutely nothing!"

"I told her. She didn't believe it, either."

"Look," he said, his breathing roughened, his voice terse and controlled, obviously losing his battle to stay calm. The heat between them rose like a fever. "I do not want to argue with you about Jessica. Not again."

"Then you probably shouldn't have kissed her," she pointed out reasonably.

"I didn't—" He broke off the denial and his fingers raked though his hair again, leaving it attractively disheveled. "I was looking everywhere for you," he explained slowly, restraining his temper with obvious effort. "Jessica snagged me and it was either dance with her or snub her, so I danced. I was walking away from her, coming to look for you, in

fact, when the new year arrived, and in the excitement, she kissed me. I forgot it even happened.
That's how unimportant it was to me.''

''Yes,'' Peyton agreed with a cool smile. ''The
unimportance is certainly what I noticed from where
I stood. I imagine that's what struck everyone else
who saw the kiss, as well.''

''Jessica is *married.*''

''So are you.''

He very nearly touched her then. His hand lifted
to within an inch of her arm, hovered there, hesitated. She stood still and breathless, yearning her
way into that touch, longing for the moment when
their anger would give way to something else, something stronger than the tension, something earthy
and elemental and wild. She nearly gave herself
away with a startled jerk when his hand dropped
abruptly back to his side.

''It's been a long week, Peyton. Tonight was a
strain for both of us. Let's not end our first night at
home in a fight.''

She wanted to fight him, pummel him with her
fists until he stopped her...and jerked her into his
arms...and kissed her senseless. ''It's a little late for
that now,'' she challenged.

''I suppose you expect an apology.''

''It's a bit late for that, too.''

The anger heated up again, rising faster now, like

water returned to the fire for a second boil. The tension escalated into vibrations as taut as violin strings and just as capable of producing sweet music. Soaring, passionate, pounding music. Until that night on Cape Cod, Peyton hadn't known it could happen like that, hadn't understood the territory they'd been traveling for months. She hadn't realized there could be a moment when everything changed, when one emotion gave way to another, and surrender was far more intriguing than making her point. She hadn't recognized that the chemistry that sparked their heated exchange of opinions fueled a desire that had been present all along, masked as aggravation and annoyance. They'd argued about Jessica that night, too. And beneath the words, which had made about as much sense at the time as these did tonight, was the red-hot attraction they both kept trying to ignore.

Well, she wasn't ignoring it tonight. Her blood pulsed with awareness and she couldn't pretend she was capable of ignoring anything about him. From the strong set of his jaw, to the dishevelment of his hair, to the way his broad chest rose and fell with agitation. Just as it had the night at the beach house. She understood what could happen this time…and no matter how much she might like to deny it, she wanted it to happen again. She wanted to *feel,* wanted to touch something tangible and real, needed to know she was still inside this body that felt lately unlike her own.

Lifting her chin, she met his eyes squarely, honestly, and saw in their midnight depths that he understood, too. For a moment—no longer than it took for a breath—their gaze held and the temptation beckoned. Her heart beat out the invitation, her cloak rustled a nervous appeal, her lips parted, waiting and ready.

But he stepped back. "Go to bed, Peyton."

She couldn't believe it. He'd argued with her, brought her to the edge…and left her hanging. "I've changed my mind."

"You've made a lot of changes this week," he said. "You need to think very long and hard before you go making another one tonight."

"I don't want to think, Matt."

He held her through the sheer persuasive power in his eyes. "Yes, you do, Peyton. Trust me. Now, go to bed. Please."

It was the *please* that did it. The genuine longing in his voice, the honest concern. He didn't want to make another mistake. He didn't want her to have another regret. So, okay, she'd go upstairs and she'd think. She owed him—and their marriage—a decent interval of consideration, she supposed, before she starting changing the rules. He was being responsible, rational, pragmatic. She could take some time to think about what she really wanted.

By the time he came upstairs to bed, she felt pretty sure she'd have reached a reasonable conclusion.

"Happy New Year, husband," she said. And turning, she left him to watch her ascent, the iridescent cloak shimmering with promises in her wake.

MATT WATCHED HER until she turned at the landing, then resolutely went back to the mail. A pointless task, as it turned out, because his mind was preoccupied with reviewing the lovely curve of her back and the intriguing sway of her hips as she'd climbed the stairs, the random flash of shapely legs he'd been able to glimpse inside the slit that ran up the back seam of her gown from the hemline to well above her knees. His inner eye traced a pleasurable vee up one shapely leg and down the other, lingering slightly at the inner curve of those knees, the glimpse of blue fabric just visible between them. A beautiful thing, he thought, that distance between, a space not even half as wide as a man's outstretched hand, and yet so tantalizing, so tempting. It was the kind of image that drove a man mad, had him wondering what was wrong with him that he'd sent her to bed alone, had him questioning what was so noble about being sensible.

She'd been inviting him to bed. No question about that. Which was not what he'd expected. Not after the evening they'd had. Not after the stress of the past week, the strain of the weeks before that. Dealing with a life-altering situation, making choices that would affect not just their futures but that of their child didn't come without considerable cost. He felt it in the tension across his neck and shoulders, the uptight, unsettled state of his nerves. Peyton had to be experiencing all that stress, plus the added strain of the physical changes taking place in her body. This was not the night for either one of them to be thinking about…well, about anything except sleep. Once she was in her room, he knew she'd be grateful he'd had the strength to resist temptation and send her to bed. Alone.

They had a year and seven months to sort out this wayward attraction, a lifetime to pay for giving in to it once. Allowing it to get the better of them now, when they were both vulnerable, wasn't smart. But knowing that didn't stop the low throb of desire from radiating heat and frustration through his body. His memory replayed the sight of her moving up the stairs, away from him, her shiny cloak rustling behind her.

Follow me. Follow me.

And he had wanted to. He had really, truly wanted to.

With a sigh, he tossed down the mail, not caring when it scattered across the credenza and several pieces fluttered to the floor. He was going to bed. That was the smart thing to do. He'd go upstairs, take a shower and get into bed.

Happy New Year, husband.

"Happy New Year, wife," he muttered as he headed up the stairs. "Happy damn New Year."

PEYTON STOOD by the door connecting her room to Matt's. The shower was still running, the rush of water in the pipes the only sound in the quiet house. Except, perhaps, for the arrhythmic beating of her heart. He'd been in the shower a long time now. Or, at least, it felt like a long time. An eternity in some ways.

She was prepared for him, ready to answer any protest he made with logical insistence. *We're married, Matt. I didn't go into this thinking it would be a platonic relationship. We're adults. Healthy adults. Given the strength of our physical attraction to each other, I'd have been an idiot to believe sex wouldn't be a part of this…arrangement. The idea must have occurred to you, too.*

Oh, yes. She had her argument all prepared. And just in case he proved difficult to convince, she'd slipped into the black silk nightie for added emphasis. It was a little tight across her breasts, which were swollen, but no longer as tender as they'd been in the first weeks of the pregnancy. Hopefully, he'd notice their rather prominent invitation first and the need for persuasion would be a moot point.

A bit nervously, she smoothed the silk for the hundredth time since she'd heard the shower start, and adjusted the neckline a little lower. *When all else fails, show more cleavage.* Michelle's advice floated from some distant past into her consciousness and she smiled. Her best friend had always been the aggressive one. Peyton had always been shy about showing any part of her ample bosom, but Michelle, who had the slim, athletic build of a gymnast, routinely bared her small cleavage to good advantage. She'd be amazed to see Peyton now, tugging at the lacy vee, pushing and prodding her breasts until they practically spilled over the top. But then, she'd be amazed to know Peyton had found a man who aroused her sexuality to the point where inhibitions foundered and willpower turned from restraint to plotting ambush.

Peyton was a little amazed herself.

But even when she heard the water shut off and her nerves kicked into overdrive, she didn't even consider not opening the door. It was as if she had no alternative but to go to him and offer herself freely. If she went to bed, she wouldn't sleep. If she slept, it would only be to dream of lying with him on passion-soaked sheets. Imagination had its place, but when reality was right next door, fantasy lost a great deal of its appeal.

Adjusting her cleavage one last time, she set her hand on the knob, gave it a twist and opened the door.

Matt entered from the bathroom at the same instant, towel-drying his hair, and unaware of her presence. Until she inhaled sharply at the sight of his nudity and the stabbing ache of desire that seized her. He looked up slowly, the towel stopped in mid-rub, and he stared at her for what surely was an eternity. Or maybe only a second. She couldn't tell, couldn't move, couldn't speak. The moment simply hovered there between them, as insubstantial as a whisper, as significant as a promise. And then, by unspoken agreement, each allowed the other's gaze to drop and then to wander at will…and with pleasure…over the body in front of them.

He was quite incredibly beautiful, Peyton decided. Damp curls dusted his chest with a defining vee of golden brown, only slightly darker than his skin. His torso was long and lean, supported by muscular thighs and calves, and his arousal was unabashedly prominent. Her eyes blinked reluctantly back to his face and caught the corner of his mouth edging into a smile.

"I think," he said huskily, "that I've been out-maneuvered."

She moistened her lips, swallowed a sudden shyness. "Well, not yet, but I'm about to give it the old college try."

His eyebrows lifted, quizzed her. "It might be easier if you came a little closer."

So he wanted her to take the final steps. She supposed that was fair. Quashing the impulse to adjust her neckline one more time, she inhaled a breath of courage, walked forward and stopped in front of him, just out of arm's reach. It wasn't uncertainty that held her there, it was anticipation. Like waiting for the first rising of the curtain before a play. She wanted to savor the moment, breathe in the scent of him, drown in the longing that swept through her in a flood of emotion. The electricity all but crackled in the air around them, that inexplicable spark of chemistry that couldn't be ignored. She'd never felt it with anyone else. The intensity, the total lack of self-consciousness, both were new to her. It was as if she saw the world in shades of gray until she got close to Matt and he brought it to blazing, vibrant color.

He held out his hands, palms up, inviting her to take the last step. Without hesitation, she did. She placed her hands in his and his confident warmth folded in around her. He moved forward as she did, meeting her halfway, his lips descending as hers lifted, and the ensuing kiss was wildly sensual…and sparked an exquisitely sweet fire. Her need for him grew instantly ravenous, and her hands would have escaped his then and wandered unimpeded over his body, except that he held her fingers laced with his and away from any other touch. His chest grazed her nipples, causing them to pebble with longing. His thighs pressed into hers, wrinkling the black silk in erotic pleats against her skin. His mouth moved over hers in demanding possession, exciting her with the play of his tongue.

And all the while, he held their hands extended slightly out and away, forcing her to feel his body only with her own, the fusion of their lips, the roughened texture of his skin brushing against the smoothness of hers, the strength of his muscular build contrasting with her womanly curves. There was more. So much more. Peyton couldn't process it all. With Matt, the sensations were almost too intense, almost too pleasurable, almost too much. *Almost.* She was hot and breathless and achy. She was eager, ardent and ambitious. She could no more control the feelings than deny them. It might be hormones, or chemistry, or pure unadulterated lust. Whatever it was, she had a comet by the tail and nothing could persuade her to let go.

She wasn't quite sure how they reached the

bed...whether he carried her or she walked, but she felt the edge of the mattress pressing against her legs, and a moment later she was sinking into its cushion, pulling Matt down with her. Or maybe he pushed her back, using their clasped hands as leverage. Her body had become so finely tuned to his touch, it was as if his thoughts were conveyed through his skin into hers, and merged with her thoughts in fluid accord. Although his weight pressed her into the mattress, covered her, possessed her and promised a sensual fulfillment, she had no concept of heaviness, felt—still—as if he would never, *could* never, be close enough. His chest against her breasts. The silky feel of chest hair teasing her nipples. His rough-soft legs tangled with hers. His sex hot and hard against her. His desire as fiery as her own. They were two, but very nearly one. They were two, but of one mind. They were two, intent on one sexual communion.

Earthy. Intense. Passionate. And beautiful.

Somehow, her hands escaped his capture—or perhaps he set them free—and traveled the slope of his back, the curve of his hips, the muscled strength of his thighs. The lusty caress of his fingers at her breast...her waist...her hips ignited small fires in its wake. His lips tasted her, taunted her, begged her, left her mouth to trail kisses down to the hollows of her throat, the sweet spot in the curve of her shoulder. He dipped lower, sought out the mounds of her breasts, the peaks of their rosy willingness. His tongue laved her to the edge of ecstasy, until she was tense with pleasure and need. His hand stroked her inner thigh until the light, almost nonexistent touch drove her mad with longing.

His breath felt as gentle on her skin as a whisper, as tantalizing as a forbidden wish. She was a banking storm, heavy with wanting, ready for release, when she twisted beneath him and maneuvered on top. Then she delivered his punishment, repaying him with long, wet kisses that brought him arching against her. She ignored his body's request for release as he had ignored hers, and tortured him with slow circles of her tongue as she moved down, discovering the territory she had explored only once before, claiming it now as her own. She neither knew nor cared if he thought her overly aggressive or wanton. She knew only the demands of this fierce, electric energy they created together. She wanted only to investigate every nuance and delight in its stunning pleasure.

At some point, Matt took command again. It could have been years later, for all the sense she had of time passing. Or a single moment. His possession was exquisitely tender, wonderfully gentle, and yet pierced her heart with its intensity. Their heartbeats, their breathing, their bodies found a common rhythm, and the passion was all that mattered, its consummation the only treasure sought.

A sigh escaped her throat. A sigh of deep pleasure. A sigh of desperate longing. And, as if he'd been waiting for it, Matt captured it on her lips, returned it, and allowed the tempest that was surrender to engulf them.

"This is a first for us," he said some long time later.

Exhausted and yet reenergized, she shifted in the crook of his arm. "What? Making love as a married couple?"

"Making love without having an argument first."

"What do you think happened downstairs?"

"That was foreplay," he said, his voice rumbling beneath her head. "Didn't you know?"

A soft smile touched her lips. "I thought that was seduction. An endeavor you rejected, I might point out."

"And which, typically, you continued until you won your point." His fingertips absently stroked the flesh of her arm. "Has anyone ever told you how stubborn you are?"

"No," she lied. "Has anyone ever said that to you?"

"No."

"You're stubborn, Matt."

"That's highly suspect coming from you, Pug."

The nickname wrapped them in an intimacy she had never anticipated and she was surprised at how much she liked it. "I'm just the only one brave enough to tell you the truth."

"No, you're not."

"Yes, I am."

"I'm sorry, but you're wrong. My sisters can be painfully blunt with me. Especially Miranda."

"My sister is blunt with me, too, but that doesn't mean her opinion isn't biased. Your sisters are the same way. They love and admire you and, therefore, they don't tell you the truth."

"Maybe they really don't believe I'm stubborn," he suggested.

"Or maybe they just know you're too stubborn to admit they might be right."

His sigh rippled beneath her, whispering across the top of her hair. "If you're spoiling for another fight, I'm afraid you're doomed to disappointment. I'm not up for another argument again quite so soon."

"Okay," she said contentedly snuggling in closer to his side. "I'll wait."

It felt good to be with him, good to be talking this way, as if they were friends. Lovers and friends. "I think this is the first time I haven't been mad at you since we met."

"Well, there was that one other time."

''I think I was mad then, too, but if it makes you feel better, I'll refer to this as the second time. Do you think that means we're becoming friends?''

''Friends who just had incredible sex?''

''Married friends who just had incredible sex.''

''Married friends who just had incredible sex and are going to be parents.''

''Hmm,'' she murmured, overwhelmed anew by the choices they'd made. ''You know what? We're doing this all backward.''

''I don't think I've ever done that before,'' he said, sounding oddly surprised by the statement. ''Working backward instead of forward, I mean.''

She turned her head to look up at him. ''I don't think I have, either.''

''Ah, a trait in common. We *are* making progress.''

A yawn caught her and the haze of sleep hovered not far behind it. ''I should go to bed,'' she said. It was one thing to lie beside him after sex, her bare body relaxed and sated next to his. It was another thing to sleep beside him until morning. That was a whole different level of intimacy and Peyton didn't want to risk being asked to leave. So she slid her legs away from his, preparatory to getting up, but he easily retrieved them, forming a sensual hook of his left leg, and sliding them back across the sheet.

"Stay," he whispered huskily, holding her gently, persuasively against his side. "Please."

It was the *please* that did it.

She stayed.

Chapter Eight

Matt parked the Mercedes and sat quietly for a moment after turning off the engine. Then his gaze swung to Peyton in the passenger seat. "I think we should tell them today," he said, his expression somber, his voice huskily sincere. "At the reception."

"No." She vetoed the idea too promptly, too sharply. "Today is Nate and Miranda's wedding day." Softening her tone, she thought she managed to sound reasonable, thoughtful. Sensible even. "We're not going to announce that we're pregnant today."

"It's time, Peyton."

She knew that. They'd kept the secret for six weeks now. She was halfway into the fourth month of the pregnancy. Her clothes no longer fastened at the waist. In another month, she wouldn't be able to disguise the hard, round bulge that would replace the flat planes of her stomach. In another month, she'd have to face the raised eyebrows, the whispers and speculation behind her back, the happy congratulations that would remind her what a fraud her marriage really was.

But she didn't have to face it today.

Not today.

"It's Miranda's day, Matt. Not ours. Let her have all the glory this once. I don't want our news to steal even one minute of it."

"We're not *stealing* anything from Miranda. She'll be happy for us. Nate will be happy for us. The whole family will be happy for us."

"But it's *their* day, Matt. Let everyone just be happy for Miranda and Nate today."

"Happiness isn't quantitative, Peyton, with only so much allotted for each occasion. This is the last time my family will be together in one place for a long time. It's the best opportunity I'm going to have to tell them all at once."

"You can tell them separately. They'll be just as happy. But today, the focus is on Miranda and Nate and I think that's exactly the way it ought to be."

His frown announced itself with a chilly sigh. "I don't want to have to make a long-distance telephone call in order to let my parents know they're going to have a grandchild. You didn't want to tell them earlier in the week because you thought they should have time to get used to the idea of our marriage. You wanted to get to know them a little first. You wanted them to get to know you. Now, they're leaving in the morning. When else will I have a chance to tell them?''

"Offer to take them to the airport and tell them then. Or tell them tonight after Miranda and Nate have left the reception.''

"That's not the way I want to do it.''

"None of this is the way you wanted to do it, Matt.'' She was edgy and more than a little rattled by his sudden resolve to make the announcement. For weeks now—six to be exact—she'd been cocooned in a lovely little fantasy world. A world in which she and Matt were lovers, honeymooners, left mostly to themselves at Danfair. A world in which she never mentioned the baby and neither did he. A world in which she pretended for lovely, uninterrupted interludes that it was the passion—that alluring, mystical, irresistible spark—that had brought them together, that kept them sharing a bed, that seemed to grow more heated and powerful with every moment they spent together. It was a world in which, for six weeks, she could pretend everything was perfect.

Under the circumstances, of course, nothing could be perfect. But still, she believed they had made real progress in their relationship. They were still too

cautious with each other, still uncertain about the
boundaries in this temporary marriage, and yet, there
were moments—quite a number of them, actually—
when she felt they were forming a true friendship.
And she wasn't ready to give up that illusion.

Not yet.

Not today.

She found a smile for him as she reached across
the console and took his hand. "Not today, Matt,"
she said. "Please?"

He looked down at her hand, ran the pad of his
thumb lightly along her skin. "They're not going to
be upset with you, Peyton, if that's what you're
afraid of. They're not going to think less of you."

Was it her imagination or had his voice laid a
definite stress on one word? *You.* They're not going
to be upset with *you.* They're not going to think less
of *you.* "I know," she said. "Your parents have
been so wonderful to me already. I honestly can't
see them getting upset about anything."

"They save their energy for better things." He
looked at her, a sadness in his eyes that she was
coming to recognize as a part of him. He was a
wonderful man, loved and respected by family and
friends. He was the kind of man people in trouble
turned to first. He was the can-do guy, the person
who could get something done, the man who ran a
foundation that truly made the world a better place.

And yet, the sadness remained, a mystery she couldn't quite get her mind around, the answer to a question she didn't know how to ask.

"I want to tell them, Peyton," he repeated. "Today."

The fear rose unbidden and formed a lump in her throat. She didn't know why she felt afraid of acknowledging publicly what she acknowledged privately every day. The baby was a fact, already a part of her life, already occupying a place in her heart, already changing her irrevocably. She knew, somehow, that the announcement would bring a change in Matt...and that's what bothered her. "Wait," she said. "Please."

The look he gave her settled the fear, eased her tension. "We'd better get inside," he said, opening his car door. "We don't want to miss the wedding. You know Miranda. Her wedding will start precisely as scheduled, with or without us." He was out of the car then, coming around to open her door, offering his hand in assistance.

Peyton took it without reservation, feeling lucky—so very lucky—to be with him.

Regardless of the circumstances...and no matter how long it lasted.

THE WEDDING WAS SMALL. Just family and a few close friends. Not at all the huge gala affair anyone who knew Miranda would have predicted. But Ainsley thought it was perfect, down to the last detail. Miranda had changed since Nate and his children had come into her life. She seemed less regimented, more flexible, simpler. And happy. Ainsley had never seen her sister wearing such a pure glow of happiness.

Pressing her shoulder into Ivan's arm as she sat beside him on the church pew, she absorbed the warmth of him, the delicious vitality of him. Happiness was contagious, she believed. Just look at her siblings. Miranda and Nate. Matt and Peyton. Andrew and Hayley—her latest successful match—who in the past six weeks had become almost inseparable. All four Danvilles had fallen in love with their perfect match. Thanks to her, Ainsley Danville Donovan, baby of the family, and apprentice matchmaker. Of course, she'd had a *little* help along the way. Ilsa. The twins. But it had been Ainsley who first saw the possibilities, and she felt she deserved to take full credit for that, if nothing else.

"Counting your blessings?" Ivan whispered, his head bending close to hers.

She nodded, smiling up at him, unable to believe anyone else in the whole world could be as happy as she. And yet, as she watched Nate slip a wedding ring onto Miranda's left hand, heard the promises they exchanged, she thought it must be possible. Because there was her sister, looking as if she'd just discovered paradise.

Ainsley had known for a long time that she wanted to be a matchmaker. She'd known in her heart she'd be good at helping people find the true treasure they sought. She'd known deep down that helping others find love was her life's calling, as meaningful in its way as her parents' humanitarian mission. Love was important. Finding a life partner gave new energy to every other purpose. Just look at Andrew. At Christmas, he'd had a broken ankle and the mistaken belief that love was something to be avoided. Then on New Year's Eve, he'd been introduced to Hayley in a whole new light and now, on Valentine's Day, his photographs reflected new depths of awareness and sensitivity that even Ainsley hadn't suspected he could reach. He'd actually documented his fall into love, photographing Hayley almost exclusively, including her even in his signature landscape portraits. Love could change the world. Ainsley believed that with her whole heart.

"It's my privilege to present to you—Mr. and Mrs. Nathaniel Shepard…and family." The minister stepped back as Miranda and Nate kissed and then gathered Cate, Will, Kali and Kori into a big hug. The older twins looked a little embarrassed, but the younger ones beamed with excitement. The small group of guests stood to applaud, and then the whole group of Shepards moved down the aisle in a happy, halting procession.

Ainsley clapped enthusiastically, caught an approving smile from Ilsa Fairchild Braddock who was sitting two rows back, and felt that she'd finally found her niche in the world, finally proved she belonged in the rather extraordinary family of her birth.

"Ready?" Ivan slipped the strap of her purse up onto her shoulder, then placed his hand at the small of her back to urge her forward. "It's time for my favorite part of the wedding."

"You can't be hungry already. You ate about a million peanuts before we got here."

"Why do you think the food is my favorite part of weddings?" he asked, trying to sound indignant. "I could have been referring to kissing the bride."

She laughed. "You could have been, but I happen to know you have the appetite of a small whale."

"But did you know that I save all my favorite kisses for you?" He pressed one to her ear. "Oh, Matt." Catching sight of his brother-in-law, he pitched his voice to reach Matt. "Would you mind if Ainsley and I rode to the reception with you and Peyton? We came early with Miranda to help with all those important, last-minute details—" He raised his eyebrows and exchanged one of those male-superior looks that indicated it was only women who were concerned with *details*. "So we have to hitch a ride to the coffeehouse."

"Sure," Matt said. "Follow me to the parking lot."

Ainsley sensed tension, noted the effort her big brother put into sounding breezy and unconcerned. She glanced at Peyton, who offered a bright smile. A too-bright smile, maybe? From the first, Ainsley had felt there was something not quite right about their elopement, something that didn't ring true about their secret romance. She'd alternated between being a little miffed that she'd missed the signs to convincing herself that Matt and Peyton had simply done a great job of keeping their private moments private. But the feeling lingered. And today, she felt as if she could reach out and touch their tension. She was suddenly certain it was not her imagination…and just as sure she had to find out what was going on and do something about it.

When it came to family, a matchmaker's work didn't necessarily end at the wedding. Sometimes, the course of true love needed a little extra assistance.

THE RECEPTION was on its last legs. The toasts had been made, the dinner eaten, the cake cut, the pictures taken, and now the adults were winding down and the kids were revving up. The deejay was reduced to playing tracks from the *Living La Vida Mickey* CD by request, and the children had long since taken over the dance floor. Kali, Kori and their buddy, Calvin Braddock, had discovered the delights of the karaoke microphone.

"Kali Shepard!" Calvin's voice blared like a seasoned newsman. "You just got married! What are you gonna do next?"

Kali took the mike. "I'm going to Disney World!" she shouted, the sound reverberating with childish energy. "Kori Shepard, you just got married! What are you gonna do next?"

"I'm going to Disney World!" Kori didn't bother with the mike. She yelled instead.

Then the two girls jumped off the dais to bounce around the dance floor like bunnies. Calvin, who was nobody's fool, regained possession of the microphone. "Calvin Braddock," he rumbled in a deep voice to an imaginary clone. "You just won the Super Bowl. What are you gonna do next?" His voice rose to a normal little-boy falsetto as he took on the other persona. "I'm going to Disney World!"

"We're going to Disney World!" The girls whooped and bunny-hopped some more.

"How much sugar do you think they've had?" Miranda asked with an unconcerned smile, her chin propped on her hand.

"At least a pound apiece," Nate said, watching

his youngest twins cavort and somersault in their frilly dresses, one pink, one red. "They're not going to sleep a wink tonight. Who's idea was it to take them to Disney World, anyway? I thought this was supposed to be our honeymoon."

"It is," Miranda laid her head against his shoulder for a minute. "First we take the whole family to Walt Disney World, then the kids go to your mother's, and you and I go off on our cruise."

"Ah, the carrot in front of the donkey's nose. So that's how you persuaded me this was a good idea."

"I think we should just count our blessings that we didn't offer to take Calvin along, too."

"Well, I'm not a complete idiot," Nate said. "Except when it comes to you."

Their smile was intimate and full of promises. Peyton looked away, feeling that simply by witnessing it she'd intruded on their privacy. Ainsley, who was sitting next to Peyton at the table, obviously had no such qualms. She was watching the newlyweds with interest, a glint of satisfaction sparkling in her eyes. Ivan, Andrew and Hayley, Linney and Charles, and Matt and Peyton filled the other seats at the round table, which was covered with a white cloth and decorated with Valentine hearts and red and pink roses. The whole Danville family, Peyton thought, her gaze traveling the circle. One set of parents, their four children, and their respective mates.

Miranda and Nate had invited a crowd to the reception, many more than had attended the small wedding, but the coffeehouse had cleared out as midnight approached, and only the die-hard friends and family were left.

Connie and Rick were still here, of course, although Scarlett had left with Covington Locke some long time ago. Peyton hadn't even attempted a protest this time. She'd had numerous run-ins with her mother lately about the wedding gift that was just waiting for an okay. The decorators were on retainer, all Peyton and Matt had to do was say yes. They kept saying no. Which aggravated Connie, which made her more determined to get her way, which kept Peyton on edge. Which only meant that she simply hadn't had the energy to fuss about the way Scarlett was allowed to run wild.

Andrew suddenly pushed back his chair and stood up, picking up his champagne glass. "I have something to say."

"Not another toast," Miranda groaned. "I'm already sloppy with good wishes."

Andy made a face at her. "Not everything is about you, Miranda," he said with a grin. "This happens to be about Hayley. And me." His eyes turned to his parents, seeking their approval and blessing. "I've asked her to marry me and, you won't believe it, but she actually said yes."

The table filled with immediate oohs and aahs, congratulations, and one enthusiastic "Yes! The matchmaker scores again!" Ainsley whooped and jumped to her feet, pumping the air with her fist. Cal Braddock picked up the action from across the room and repeated it into the microphone, which sent Kali and Kori bouncing and tumbling wildly around the dance floor, giggling uncontrollably. The irresistible sound of children laughing proved contagious and soon everyone had joined into the spirit of celebration.

Linney and Charles got up to embrace Hayley, welcoming her to the Danville family with the same graciousness they'd offered Peyton earlier in the week. Somehow the memory brought a mist of tears to her eyes, a wistful smile to her lips. Lately, hormonal surges zapped her energy and left her weepy. Or maybe it was simply the knowledge that she was deceiving this wonderful family. Matt's hand brushed her shoulder and lingered at her back as he stood, too. "I have an announcement to make, as well."

Peyton realized what he was going to say too late to stop him.

Of course, she couldn't have stopped him any more than she could stop the life events her choices had already set into motion. She wasn't ready for this moment, and yet, she didn't know why the announcement seemed so momentous—perhaps because it was so irrevocable, perhaps because it deepened the deception, added another layer to her guilt. But ready or not, here it came.

"Mom. Dad." Matt lifted his glass to them, then to the next table over, where Peyton's parents sat. "Connie. Rick. Congratulations, you're going to be grandparents!"

Peyton's heart sank even as she revived her smile to reflect a happiness she wanted desperately to feel. She did her part, as she had done for the past six weeks. She held Matt's hand in a death grip and pretended that the only thought in her head was her incredible good fortune. A husband. A baby. A future filled with the kind of love and acceptance this family gave so freely.

She was hugged and patted, coddled and crooned over, but Matt deflected any questions as easily as he seemed to do most everything else. He held her close to his side, protectively, lovingly, as if she was the most precious gift in his life, and Peyton realized that under a different set of circumstances, this would have been one of the happiest times of her life.

But she knew, even if no one else suspected, that Matt's arm around her was there for the sake of appearances. His smile singled her out only because others were there to notice. His laughter was warm and genuine only because he wanted to convey to everyone present that everything was right in his world.

And Peyton understood suddenly that he was totally convincing because he'd been playing a role all his life. She'd watched him at the Foundation, seen the way he adjusted his demeanor to fit the expectation of whatever situation confronted him. He'd been juggling responsibility of one sort or another his entire life. Charles and Linney were truly wonderful people, selfless and committed, and yet they had sacrificed being present in their children's lives for what they perceived to be the greater good. As the oldest, the firstborn of his generation, Matt had naturally taken up the role vacated by his father—head of the family, head of the Foundation, expected to be as selfless in his roles as his parents were in theirs. No wonder she felt at times that he was soul weary and simply going through the motions of living.

"Are you okay?" Matt leaned down to whisper in her ear, his breath warm against her face. "You look…pale."

Was he really concerned? Or simply reminding her that she, too, had a role to play tonight? "Fine," she said, seeing him in a different light, seeing everything from a whole new perspective. "Just fine."

And then she smiled at him. A real smile. A smile meant to cut through his defenses and touch his heart. A smile that said everything was right in her world and that, somehow, she was going to make everything right in his world, as well.

His hand tightened at her waist and he leaned in to brush a kiss across her lips. Her body responded as it always did to his touch—with instant, embarrassing heat—and his body answered in kind. That part of their relationship, at least, was real. Even as accomplished an actor as Matt obviously was couldn't fake the passion that virtually possessed them behind closed doors. They had that…and a baby on the way.

There was no reason to feel guilty about the choices they'd made. They were adults. They were married. And although she hated to admit her mother might have been right, Peyton thought perhaps change was exactly what Matt needed in his life. And change was one thing she was confident she could provide. "I've never been so happy," she said softly, just for him to hear…and ponder.

It wasn't the truth yet, but it would be soon. Very soon.

"This is so exciting," Ainsley said, her dimples flashing with her pleasure. "Another wedding and a baby. Mom, Dad, you're going to be making more trips home.''

Andrew agreed with a nod. "Since Ainsley got married at Halloween, Matt after Christmas, and now Miranda at Valentine's Day, Hayley and I thought we'd carry on the holiday tradition and get married on the Fourth of July.''

"That doesn't give us much time to plan," Miranda said, clearly already thinking ahead. "Of course, it's more time than Ainsley and Ivan gave me." She turned to Hayley. "And it won't hurt my feelings if you and Andrew want to plan the whole thing yourselves.''

"Give us a break, Miranda." Ainsley laughed. "Hayley, take my advice and let her take care of all the details. Otherwise she'll drive Andrew nuts reminding him to remind you to take care of them.''

"You forget, Baby, that I'm a changed woman." Miranda snuggled her hand in Nate's, gave him that private smile again. "I have a family of my own now and the rest of you will have to manage your own details from now on.''

The family's laughter was good-humored, if skeptical, of her new philosophy.

"So," Linney said approvingly. "We'll have another wedding in July and a baby in the fall.''

Peyton felt Matt tense beside her, and stepped in to rescue him from himself. "A little sooner than that, actually,'' she said, casting Matt an I'll-handle-this smile. "Matt and I have done things a bit backward. A first for both of us.'' She squeezed his hand, trying to ease his tension. "The baby might even be here in time for the wedding.''

If that surprised anyone, it didn't show. There was simply another round of excited comments, some discussion from Miranda—mostly with herself—about whether to schedule the baby shower before the wedding shower or vice versa, and a few questions to Peyton about how she was feeling, if she'd found a doctor, and if she'd had an ultrasound. It was a subject most interesting to the women, a subject that didn't exclude the men, but left them unsure how, and if, they wanted to be included. Nate was the only one of the men to venture a comment. "It could be twins,'' he said. "They run in the family, you know.''

"Not in my family they don't.'' Peyton laughed and realized it felt good. Genuinely good. She had absorbed Matt's worry these past weeks, worried about what someone else might think, allowed his expectations that he would somehow disappoint his family to rob her of the pleasure of anticipation. The arrival of this baby—hers and Matt's—should be anticipated with wonder and the expectation of joy. No matter what the circumstances of conception, she wanted this baby. She believed Matt did, too.

It was time for him to realize that their *mistake* held the possibility of more blessings than his heart could hold.

And it was time for her to admit she was falling in love with the man—and the life—she had so unexpectedly chosen.

Chapter Nine

Jessica walked into Matt's office without knocking and closed the door behind her.

Not a good sign.

"Jessica," he said coolly. "What can I do for you?"

She sat across from him, in one of the chairs in front of his desk, and crossed her legs, the split in her skirt draping conveniently to show her assets to best advantage. "I've postponed this as long as I can, Matthew, and I hate to be the one to do it, but we have to talk about Peyton."

He'd been expecting this, but hoping Jessica would have the good sense not to put him in this position. Apparently, that had been too much to hope for. "Peyton, my *wife?*" He stressed the word, wanting her to understand where he stood before she started.

"Don't be that way, Matthew. You know I'd

never come to you with this if it wasn't absolutely necessary. But when it affects the Foundation, I feel you must be informed.''

He settled back in his chair, offering no encouragement, knowing she needed none. She'd been advocating for this discussion from the minute she'd found out Peyton was pregnant, had been pregnant before they married. Matt wasn't a fool. He knew Jessica had disliked Peyton from the start, had championed her only to create conflict and reveal her for the Louisiana rube she thought Peyton must be. Anyone hailing from below the Mason-Dixon Line was suspect to Jessica. Being nouveau riche, as the O'Reillys undeniably were, made it worse. Add to that the possessive attitude she had mistakenly adopted toward him and that Matt couldn't seem to dispel, and he'd known they were headed for trouble.

Which wouldn't have mattered under different circumstances.

But, with the well-honed instincts of a coquette, Jessica had seen Peyton as competition long before he had admitted the attraction to himself. He knew he was correct in believing Jessica thought he'd been tricked into this marriage. And, from the glint of steel in her eyes, he could see now that she meant to rescue him.

Pulling the fabric modestly over her knee, she adjusted the front slit of her skirt, only to have it fall open again, revealing even more of her shapely thigh. "You know, of course, Matthew, that I haven't been happy with the way she's handled the Black-and-White Ball almost from the beginning. But, as you have pointed out on other occasions, I am the one who cast the deciding vote in her favor and handed her the event chair. She seemed such an enthusiastic volunteer, I truly believed she deserved the opportunity to prove herself."

Her pause was merely for effect, although her pretty frown made it seem as if she was struggling to find the right words. "No one has been more surprised than I at how poorly she's handled the responsibility. I know she's your wife, and even if she wasn't, I understand—probably better than any-one—that it is not the policy of this foundation to criticize its volunteers. Especially those with deep pockets…and the O'Reillys have been very gener-ous."

He said nothing, just waited for her to go on.

"But Olivia Renwick has served on our advisory board for years and has chaired the Black-and-White Ball more times than anyone can recall, and done an absolutely splendid job each and every time. She's a major contributor to this event, as well as various other fund-raisers, every single year and, re-gardless of our personal feelings, her opinion has to be considered, Matthew. We can't afford to offend her over something as trivial as table decorations.''

Table decorations. Some days—a lot of days, actually—he really hated this job. ''It's the Black-and-White Ball,'' he said wearily. ''The tables are covered in black-and-white cloths and the centerpieces are a variety of white flowers in black-and-white vases. What did Peyton do to offend Mrs. Renwick? Order a few white carnations to mix in with the white orchids?''

''She didn't order floral arrangements at all,'' Jessica replied with a certain zealous satisfaction. ''She decided—without even running the idea by me, much less the advisory board—that the money was wasted—she actually used the word *wasted*—on flowers, so she cut centerpieces from the event budget.''

''I hope she didn't cut the linen budget, too,'' he said facetiously. ''I can't imagine the uproar it would cause if she wanted to do away with the tablecloths.''

''It isn't funny, Matthew. When the advisory board discovered what she'd done and tried—very nicely, I might add—to suggest she reconsider her decision, *she* suggested that if the board wanted centerpieces on the tables, they should consider making some inexpensive decorations as a group project.'' Jessica looked properly appalled. ''She actually said *group project* to women who have collectively contributed millions of dollars over the years to the Danville Foundation.''

Personally, Matt thought the word *inexpensive* had probably been the more offensive, especially in the view of the extravagant and excessively fussy Olivia. ''And that's why Mrs. Renwick is on the warpath,'' he said just to clarify the issue.

''Don't underestimate her, Matthew. She feels she's suffered a major insult and that her past service is unappreciated.''

''That's ridiculous.''

''Peyton is *your* wife, Matthew. How she handles herself is now a direct reflection on you and on the Danville Foundation. You have to deal with this problem now, while it can still be salvaged. Peyton doesn't understand how to deal with people in this stratum of society. It isn't her fault, of course, that her background offered no experiences that could have prepared her for this type of situation. But that doesn't alter the fact that our patrons expect a certain amount of respect and deference for their position in society and that regardless of her personal opinion, it is her responsibility as a Danville to see that these individuals receive the homage they've earned.''

''Inherited, you mean.''

''No, that isn't what I mean. They've absolutely

earned special consideration because of their generous support of the Foundation through fund-raisers like the Black-and-White Ball and through the quite significant clout they bring to our boards.''

She was right. Over the years, Matt had run smack into the wall of influence that women such as Olivia Renwick wielded with queenly disregard for practicality. To the Olivias of the world, self-importance trumped common sense, and centerpieces of exotic, expensive orchids were as integral to a successful event as identifying who was wearing last year's fashion. However trivial he found this latest uproar, he knew it had to be handled. And he knew Olivia had to carry the day. ''I'll talk to Peyton,'' he said.

''You have to do more than that, Matthew. She's irritated everyone with her insistence that event budgets are outrageous and that past fund-raisers would have been far more successful if expenses had been slashed to the bone. This is no longer about orchids in the flower arrangements. Olivia's threatening to skip the ball and withdraw her standing commitment to future events. If she does that, we'll lose Natalie Bonner and the Gardner sisters, too. That's four of our largest individual contributors and, very possibly, there will be others who'll follow Olivia's lead. In this economy, that could cause cuts in funding for services. I don't believe you want that, Matthew.

Especially not when there's something you can do to prevent it.''

''Ask Peyton to order flower arrangements?'' But he knew that wasn't Jessica's aim even before she corrected him.

''It's too late for conciliatory gestures. Peyton needs to step down as event chair.''

''The ball is barely a week away,'' he pointed out.

''I'll step in and smooth things over. I'll have to work day and night to do it, but this late in the game, there really isn't any alternative.''

So she expected him to instruct Peyton to step aside and turn the event over to her. Peyton had been working on the Black-and-White Ball for nearly a year and Matt thought it was grossly unfair to force her out now. But Jessica was right. At this point, there was no other choice. ''I'll talk to her,'' he said. ''Is there anything else?''

Jessica looked at him as if contemplating what she wanted to say. ''There's a lot of talk about your marriage,'' she stated finally. ''You know I despise gossip, but considering your position with the Foundation, I think you need to know what people are saying. The rumor going around is that Peyton and that mother of hers set out to entrap you and that the baby probably isn't even yours.''

He snapped forward in the chair and pushed to his feet. ''I won't dignify that with a response,'' he replied sharply. "Now, if you have no other *business* to discuss with me, this meeting is over."

She stood, slowly, smoothing the front of her skirt. One thing about Jessica, she never pushed too hard at any one time. Chinese water torture was more her style. "This has to be done today, you know. The Black-and-White Ball is Saturday evening. That's only four days from now. I assume you'll want me to take charge of the arrangements immediately?"

Of course, she would insist that he verbally hand over the authority even before he'd talked to Peyton. "Yes, Jessica. Do whatever you feel must be done."

"Thank you, Matthew." She walked to the door, paused with her hand on the knob, looked back at him with an expression of deep understanding. "I want you to know you can talk to me. About anything. Anytime. I'll always be here for you."

She walked out then, leaving him angry and resigned. Once again, he had to set aside his personal feelings for the good of the Foundation. But for the first time, he was going to have to explain his decision to someone else. To Peyton. And there wasn't a doubt in his mind about her reaction. She wouldn't take this sitting down.

He might as well prepare himself for one hell of a fight.

MATT DIDN'T KNOW when or exactly what had happened, but sometime in the month since Miranda's wedding, he'd begun looking forward to going home. Something was different.

No, actually, a lot was different.

Peyton was redecorating Danfair, for one thing. She'd asked Charles and Linney for their permission and opinions. She'd checked and double-checked with Andrew, Ainsley and Miranda. She'd asked Matt point-blank if he wanted her to leave the house exactly as it was or if she could make a few changes. As everyone else had given an enthusiastic thumbs-up, he could hardly be the lone holdout, so he'd told her to do anything she wanted, although he'd prefer she didn't go around knocking down walls.

That had made her laugh.

The laughter was new, too. He'd noticed her laughing a lot this past month. She was different, somehow. Her eyes sparkled, her smile came easily and often, and her skin seemed to emit a happy glow of health. He'd even heard her singing to herself in a soft, pleasant alto. No matter what her schedule during the day, she was almost always home when he returned, and she greeted him with what certainly appeared to be genuine pleasure. And in ways he couldn't yet define, Danfair had begun to feel like a home again.

An intangible shift had occurred in her relationship with her mother, too, it seemed. The tension between them hadn't gone away, but it no longer felt like a ticking time bomb, either. He'd arrived home several times to find the two women engaged in companionable conversations, comparing paint samples and fabrics. Scarlett had been with them on a few occasions and had actually made an effort to be pleasant while giving him her opinion—most often, a yawn—about Danfair's new look. If it had been *her* house, she'd informed him, she'd have made it much more *interesting,* a concept that seemed to involve sculpted furniture, fluorescent lighting and a lot of black paint. Matt had told her he thought she might have a future as a decorator, which won him a few good-brother-in-law points even though it appeared to cost him a couple of points with his mother-in-law. He never ran into one of Connie's pet decorators at the house, but he felt sure they had a finger in the planning pie somewhere behind the scenes.

Matt battled mixed feelings about the O'Reillys paying for a major overhaul of his family home, but it seemed to make Peyton happy to be doing this and so he made peace with the gift for her sake. She went out of her way to consult with him on everything, paint, repairs, even something as minor as cleaning a set of drapes. His answer to her was consistent…whatever she wanted to do was okay with him.

So Danfair slowly evolved from a playground back into the courtly estate it had once been. The indoor croquet field disappeared and all the old wood floors were sanded and buffed to a rich, aged sheen. The dining room had been freshly painted a soft gray, the crayoned drawings of years past covered by who knew how many coats of primer. The mural on the ceiling looked newly clean, and the chandelier, cracked and out of balance for years because of a stray football, had been restored. The table, which had been brought from France as a wedding gift for his paternal great-grandmother, was polished to a mirrored shine and, although the two antique hutches and long buffet weren't matches in period or style, they looked as if they belonged in the room. At some point, Miranda had suggested Peyton should check the attic for furniture that had been stored over the years rather than left out to bear the use and abuse of four rowdy youngsters. So new-old pieces seemed to appear magically while Matt was at the office.

He hadn't said anything to Peyton, but he liked the changes, liked walking through a house that felt as if it was growing up and into a comfortable adulthood. It was like a game to stroll from one room to another, discovering what—or if—new changes had occurred during his day's absence. But most of all, he looked forward to wandering through the house until he found Peyton, either finishing up, or still immersed in, her latest project.

Today he discovered her alone in her bedroom, standing between the two windows, leaning slightly against the wall and observing the room with a calculating eye. Her dark hair was caught loosely at the back of her head and held by a big, toothy clip. He imagined her pushing it out of her face and up off her neck—as he'd watched her do any number of times—before finally, hastily, grabbing the clip and securing it out of her way. She was wearing one of his shirts over a pair of stretch pants, and her bare toes periodically scrunched down into the nap of the carpet. The pregnancy showed now in a slight roundness that couldn't be concealed even beneath the oversize shirt. He smiled, glad he was home.

"What are you thinking about so hard?" he asked.

She blinked and turned toward him with a guilty grin. "Hello, Matt," she said…and the warmth in her voice felt like music. "I was just imagining how this will look as a nursery. This room seems the obvious choice since it connects to yours."

"And since you haven't spent a single night in it."

A slight blush crept into her cheeks, but she met

his eyes—and his thoughts—with bold challenge, daring him to say he'd have it any other way. Which, of course, he wouldn't. Her presence and warmth in his bed every night was an unexpected bonus, what Peyton referred to as a little Louisiana lagniappe. His bedroom had evolved into *their* bedroom without either one of them saying a word. But he supposed that wasn't quite true. He'd said, "Stay," and she'd stayed.

"I think this room must have been a nursery initially, don't you? Imagine that, Matt. One of your ancestors, maybe several of them, could have occupied this room as a baby. And in a few months your son will sleep and dream here. Doesn't that give you goose bumps just to think about it?"

He couldn't say it did, but her eyes sparkled, and when she gave him that smile, he was ready to agree with anything she said. "I can see our little girl in this room," he said, letting his gaze travel the length of the room and back again. "We should paint it pink. A nice feminine pink."

"I'm thinking blue. A bright, little-boy blue. With, maybe, a pirate-ship mural on that wall. In tribute to old Black Dan."

He shook his head. "We don't want her growing up as too much of a tomboy. Let's go with unicorns and a princess or two."

"Don't be silly. He'll want pirates not princesses."

Peyton smiled then. So did he. They'd begun to talk about the baby. She was certain it was a boy. He was adamant it was a girl. So they engaged in this friendly game of debate over their child's gender. "Peyton," he said impulsively. "Let's go out for dinner. Just the two of us. Somewhere quiet."

Her eyebrows lifted with interest. "Somewhere romantic?"

"If you like."

She came across the room to him, smelling like new paint and cinnamon toast, which had turned out to be the one food she craved. Coming up on tiptoe, she kissed him lightly on the lips. "You've got yourself a date. I'll need an hour to get ready."

"I'll wait." And at that moment, he thought he must have been waiting for her all his life.

THE LITTLE RESTAURANT in Jamestown lay off the beaten track. It was quiet with soft and romantic light. The music floated unobtrusively around them, adding atmosphere but not distraction. The food was simple and superb, the service attentive and inconspicuous. Peyton loved every minute of their date, wished it wouldn't end, longed to capture the relaxed, happy rhythms of their conversation in her memory so she could remember the ease of it whenever she liked.

Matt seemed different tonight. He looked at her differently. He was relaxed and comfortable, as if theirs was an old and treasured friendship. The everpresent spark of attraction between them felt like part of a larger whole, as if it were just the bass notes in a symphony and not the only part of the melody that was their relationship. They had done this all backward, she thought again. The sizzle had brought them together, two strangers, who were now—months after their marriage—falling in love with the lover they were just coming to know.

"Now what are you thinking about?" he asked, his gaze soft and affectionate.

"What makes you so sure I'm thinking about anything except how much I ate?"

"It's the tilt of your lips, Peyton. It gives you away every time."

She tried to suppress the tilt, but it was disobliging and tipped farther toward a smile. "Well, if you must know, I was thinking about doing things backward and that had I known things could turn out so well, I might have tried this technique in other areas of my life before now."

"You think this—*us*—is turning out well?" He seemed a bit hesitant, almost anxious that he might have misinterpreted her remark. "Really?"

"Yes, I really think this—*us*—is turning out amazingly well. Don't you?"

"I honestly hadn't given it much thought before, but lately…" He reached for her hand, which had settled on the tabletop, and covered it with his own. "You're different, Peyton. I don't know what it is, but you've changed, and I…well, I like it."

"Me, too." She decided to tell him, wanted suddenly to share the change in her perspective. "You remember the night of Miranda's wedding? Well, of course you do. I was miserable…so worried when you told everyone about the baby. I guess I thought we could keep it a secret indefinitely. But once you'd said it, I saw nothing but happiness and excitement in your parents' and sisters' faces. Even Andrew looked pleased at the idea of being an uncle. And suddenly I realized that I'd spent all this time worrying about what other people would think, believing that getting pregnant by accident was something shameful and sad. That's the way I'd framed the scene in my mind, picturing disappointment behind every smile, the undertones of reproach in every voice. That's the reason—or one of the reasons—I wanted us to be married. I didn't want the taint of illegitimacy for the baby, but I didn't want it for me, either. I thought marriage was the right thing, that it would protect me from the feeling I'd made a terrible mistake and embarrassed both of our families.''

Turning his hand over, she stroked the lines in his palm with a gentle fingertip. ''My mother grew up dirt poor, ashamed of her family and the life she left behind. She never looked back and she's never talked about it. That's why she's so conscious of status, so concerned about appearances and what others think of her, of Scarlett, of Dad, of me. I'd probably never have known anything about her childhood if Dad hadn't always been so proud of her determination and grit. He thinks she's courageous and wonderful, but even after all these years, she still doesn't believe that. She's more embarrassed by the past she came out of than where she is today.

''When you announced we were having a baby, it suddenly hit me like a brick that I'd grown up absorbing her sense of shame, the way she bases her worth on her perception of what someone else thinks about her. Just like her, I was concentrating on how my actions would appear to other people. I realized I expected to be criticized not congratulated. I believed I deserved disapproval, not the happy acceptance I received instead. It may not make much sense to you, Matt, coming from the background and the family you have, but children learn more from what is *never* said than from the most often repeated values. My mother said one thing, but her actions and reactions taught me something else entirely. She believes money can buy her the acceptance she needs. I thought I could earn acceptance by never making a mistake. Somehow, in that instant at the reception, I suddenly understood it was my choice to consider this baby a blessing or a foolish, unforgivable mistake." She met his blue, blue eyes. "So I chose the blessing."

"And that has made you happy." His voice sounded a little husky and his fingers closed around hers once again. "I'm glad."

"Me, too," she whispered. "I hope my change of attitude has made you a little happier, too."

"A lot happier," he said. "And, believe it or not, my life hasn't been as perfect as you might think. The Danvilles have our share of secrets, too, you know."

"Tell me one, Matt. Tell me something about you that no one else knows. Please?"

His thumb brushed absently across her hand and his gaze dropped to study the top of the table. She thought he was withdrawing, that he wasn't inclined to share anything personal with her because he didn't trust her enough. But after a few minutes... what seemed like very long minutes...he looked up with a slight, offhand shrug. "I've always resented my parents for the choices they made. Pretty selfish, huh?''

Her eyes misted with sympathy. ''I don't think so, Matt. Your parents are wonderful, generous people, but that doesn't mean they didn't make their share of mistakes.''

''I'm not going to do that with my child,'' he said.

She offered a soft smile. ''We'll make mistakes, Matt. We just have to do our best not to make big ones.''

''Then we should definitely paint the nursery pink.''

The curve of his lips made her pulse race. She was so in love with him, her heart ached with the pleasure of it and she almost—*almost*—told him so. ''It's a boy, Matt,'' she said instead. ''I just feel it.''

He withdrew his hand and picked up his wineglass, tipping it toward her in a salute. ''You've been wrong before,'' he replied, taking a drink. ''Do you want anything else before we go? Coffee? Dessert? I'll bet they make pretty good cinnamon toast here.''

''No, thank you. I've already gained thirteen pounds and I'm barely halfway through the pregnancy. I'm afraid I'm not even going to fit into my dress for Saturday's ball.''

He set the glass down, exhaled slowly. ''I talked with Jessica today. She's going to step in and take over the last of the arrangements so you can relax and just enjoy the event.''

A chill of annoyance trickled like ice water down her back, robbing her pleasure in the evening. ''Jessica is assuming my duties as chair of the Black-and-White Ball?''

A guilty expression flitted across his face and was gone. But she'd seen it. And she knew.

''It was my decision, Peyton. I thought it would be best.''

''Because you discovered I'm incompetent?''

''Of course not.''

''No, of course you didn't.'' She knew the source of this decision, suspected she knew the gist of the evidence against her. What she didn't understand was why Matt hadn't given her even the benefit of the doubt. ''Because we both know I'm very competent and that I've done a damn good job in planning this event.''

''I had what I believe to be valid reasons for my decision. Let's leave it at that.''

''No. I want an answer. A real one. Not excuses.''

''I don't make excuses.'' He placed his napkin beside his plate with unwarranted emphasis. ''You're out as event chair. Jessica's in. I made the decision and I stand by it.''

She narrowed her eyes. ''That's what's behind this whole date night, isn't it, Matt? You brought me out to a public place, softened me up with a good meal, a lot of small talk and a pseudo exchange of personal secrets, just so I wouldn't make a scene. Tell me, Matt, was this Jessica's idea, too? Did you and she discuss the best way to inform me of your nasty little plot? Or did you think of this *romantic* evening all on your own?''

''As usual, Peyton, you're making a big deal out of something that isn't that complicated.''

She tossed her napkin onto her plate and leaned forward, her hands gripping the edge of the table, her voice low but forceful. ''And, as usual, Matt, you're willing to believe anything Jessica tells you.''

''I'm not going to discuss this with you here.''

''You have no intention of discussing it with me anywhere. We've been having this same argument almost from the first minute I began volunteering at the Foundation, and it is always about Jessica. No matter what the problem, it somehow always comes back to her. You never question her, never consider that someone else could legitimately view the situation from a different perspective, never allow yourself to believe there could be any other interpretation of what she chooses to tell you.''

''Jessica is an employee who is paid to do exactly what she does.''

''Oh, really. You hired her to ensure that a handful of bigoted old women are allowed to ridicule every new idea presented to their so-called *advisory* board? You hired her to stand back while new volunteers are humiliated for daring to suggest it may be time to change the way things have always been done? You hired her to inflame a minor disagreement into a raging tantrum of wounded pride and imagined insults? Because that is what Jessica does. That's why the Foundation has lost some valuable volunteers in the past several months. Women like Judy Statton and Lindy Howard, Audra Rey and Tracy Moore. And those are just the ones I personally know about. They took their volunteer hours, their donations and their energies to other nonprofit organizations because they have a lot to offer and they were stifled and unappreciated at your foundation. It may be true they don't have the financial resources of Olivia Renwick or Natalie Bonner or the Gardners at this time in their lives, but in a few years they will. So you've not only lost their enthusiasm and the vitality they have to give, you've lost their future contributions.'' She pushed back and stood up, angry with herself for believing he'd changed, for thinking he was going to allow her to participate in this relationship as a partner. ''And now, Matt, you've lost me, too.''

He was also angry as he rose to his feet. ''This whole uproar is about table decorations, Peyton. *Table decorations!* Do you know how much I hate that? Do you have any idea how many times I've been caught in a squabble like this over something as stupid and unimportant as whether or not there are flowers on the tables?''

"I thought you loved the Danville Foundation, Matt. I thought it was possibly the only thing you did truly care about. And yet, after everything I've just said, you still want to pretend this is about trivialities. That isn't leadership, Matt. That's denial. If you don't want to make the tough choices, then step back and let someone else do it. But don't tell me that the decision you made today was based on anything more than the fact that you don't want to be bothered with the truth.'' She shook her head, knowing she was either going to start crying or go around the table and kick him, hard, on the shin. As neither action would do anything other than irritate him further and upset her more, she held out her hand expectantly. "May I have the car keys, please?''

He wasn't through arguing his point. She could see that, but she was through. She wasn't going to fight him over a charity event. She wasn't going to fight him at all. Not anymore. Their gaze held for a moment, the air sparked with tension and energy, pulsed with unspoken emotion, and then he reached into his pocket and handed her the keys. "I'll be out as soon as I've taken care of the bill," he said.

She didn't bother to answer, just picked up her

purse, draped her cardigan across her shoulders and walked out of the restaurant. Before he ever even came out the door, she was already on her way across the Newport Bridge.

MATT COULD NOT BELIEVE she'd driven off without him. But the evidence was irrefutable. The Mercedes and Peyton were gone. Not even a set of taillights flickering in the distance. She must have driven out of there like a bat out of hell. Jamming his hands into his pockets, he decided he'd call a cab.

But first, he was going back inside the restaurant to order a stout drink. Maybe two. After all, why hurry? There was nothing at home for him but more argument. And frankly, between Jessica and Peyton, he'd had his fill of tempests in teapots.

Turning on his heel, he abandoned the parking lot and returned to the restaurant in search of some liquid consolation.

PEYTON NEVER EVEN SAW the car that hit her.

One minute she was telling Matt—in absentia—that he was an idiot, and the next a flash of headlights was coming toward her out of nowhere.

An instant of awareness—no longer than a pair of heartbeats—before the crash, the horrendous *pow!* of collision.

And then…nothing.

Chapter Ten

Matt paid the driver and walked toward the house, considerably worse for the wear of having replayed the argument over and over in his head while his whiskey sour sat untouched on the bar. Only when the front door was flung open before he reached it did he realize the house was blazing with lights, charged with intangible tensions.

"Matt!" Ainsley grabbed his arm and jerked him inside. "Where have you been? Why didn't you answer your cell phone? What were you doing out so late? Are you hurt? Were you in the car? What happened to you?"

He sobered quickly from what little alcohol he'd actually consumed. "Slow down, Baby. I'm fine. What's going on?"

"There was an accident, just this side of the bridge."

Fear gripped him. "Peyton?" He could barely breathe the question, couldn't find the words to ask.

"At the hospital," Ainsley answered. "Ivan's with her. That's all I know. The police called here first, but all Frederico could understand was that they wanted a phone number...so he gave them mine. We thought you were in the car, too, and that you must have been thrown out in the crash, although I told the police you always wear your seat belt and I didn't see how you could have just disappeared. They're probably out there searching for you still. We'll have to call and let them know you showed up." She paused for breath, barely. "Where were you anyway? And why was Peyton driving home alone?"

Matt stopped listening. "Where's your car?" he asked.

She divined his intention and grabbed the car keys before he could. "You're in no condition to drive," she said, running ahead of him outside to where her car was parked. "Get in."

The tires couldn't have turned more than three times before Ainsley was at him again with the questions. "What happened, Matt? How did you get to Danfair? Do you realize it's nearly two o'clock in the morning? Why was Peyton out so late? Was she with you? Why weren't you with her? Oh, how could this have happened? You can tell me, Matt. You can tell me anything.''

"Women keep saying that to me," he said, because he was scared, because the thought flitted through his mind and came out his mouth. Ainsley was scared, too, hence her babbling. He inhaled a shaky breath and made himself focus. "I don't know what happened, Ainsley, except that she drove off without me. I guess she was heading back here, but I don't know. She could have been going anywhere.''

"So you went out looking for her?"

He frowned. "No. I went back inside the restaurant and ordered a drink.''

"What restaurant?"

"The one where we had dinner.'' His fingers drummed nervously on the armrest.

"Oh, you had dinner.''

"That's what I just said.''

"No, you said you went looking for Peyton after she drove off without you.''

Sometimes he wondered if women ever actually listened to what a man said. "No, I *said,* she drove off in a huff and left me at the restaurant," he repeated. "I went back inside and sat at the bar for a while, then I called a taxi and went home.''

"A huff?'' Ainsley tossed a glance at him, gripped the wheel as if her life—or maybe Peyton's—depended on it. "What did you do to put her in a huff?"

"I didn't do anything," he snapped, feeling as guilty as sin. "Why does it have to be *my* fault?"

"Oh, for heaven's sake, Matt. Talk to me. For once in your life, let someone help you."

He looked at her then, her gold hair muted in the darkness inside the car, her expression drawn taut with worry, and he wondered when she'd grown up and why it was difficult for him to accept that. He'd always thought he'd played the role of big brother just right, giving his siblings the proper amount of protective concern, telling them they had nothing to worry about, pretending he never felt weighted down with the responsibility he carried. But maybe he'd gotten that all wrong, too. Maybe Ainsley thought she'd been a burden to him. Maybe she'd grown up believing her role was to make him smile and laugh, to pretend she had no worries so she never added to his. Maybe she'd absorbed a message from him that he'd never meant to send. "What did you think of me when you were younger, Baby?"

Her eyebrows drew together in a frown. "I've always thought you were wonderful. You know that."

"But what else? The truth, Ains. Not just what you think I want to hear."

The frown softened and she chewed on her lower

lip for a minute or two while she contemplated the answer. "I thought you were strong. And handsome. I thought you were wise and a little stern. I thought you never laughed enough. I thought you didn't really like to talk very much and that you always had something important on your mind." She paused, cast him a worried glance. "But mostly I thought you were sad and often lonely, even when we were with you."

So much for thinking no one had ever seen past his facade. "And now?"

"Now? I think you're still sad. I think you're still lonely. I think you have a chance to change that. But I don't know if you're going to take it."

What if that chance was gone? Snatched back before he could claim it. *Now, Matt, you've lost me, too.* Tears ached behind his eyes and gathered into a knot of pain in his throat. He swallowed hard and turned his head toward the window and the darkness beyond it.

Ainsley took a hand from the wheel to touch him with comfort. "She's going to be all right, Matt. She is."

She had to be. He couldn't bear it if she wasn't. "The baby," he said then, suddenly realizing what else was at stake. "Is the baby…?" He couldn't finish the sentence, couldn't ask, couldn't believe he might lose what he'd only so recently realized he truly wanted.

Ainsley bit her lip again. "There's some concern about the baby, Matt. That's all I know."

The ache became unbearable. Fear seized his heart and crushed it in a vise of terrifying possibilities. "I love her," he said, not knowing until that moment that he did.

Ainsley gently squeezed his arm. "I know you do. After all, I am a matchmaker."

PEYTON CAME AWAKE slowly, aware of an overall ache that seemed to have settled deep into every muscle of her body. Her eyes drifted open to take in the sterile drabness of a hospital room. The starchy bleached linens felt cool beneath the exploratory movements of her fingertips. There was a hum of machinery somewhere nearby, a rustle of movement beyond her vision. She remembered a doctor in green scrubs who'd asked her name and what day it was. She remembered telling him—or someone—she was pregnant. Five months, she thought she'd said. And then... The memories blurred again at that point, blipped off into some distant galaxy of forgetfulness.

Her hand slid to her stomach, searching and thankfully finding the firm bulge that meant the baby was still there. She pushed at it and felt the flutter of his kick. He was okay. She sighed and turned her head on the pillow.

Matt was asleep in a chair, pulled up close to the bed, his head propped on one hand but still drooping toward his chest. He'd have one heck of a pain in his neck when he awoke, she thought. Just looking at him made her feel better, so she lay there and watched him sleep while the baby moved inside her. She must have dozed off again, because when she opened her eyes for the second time, Matt was standing by the window, looking out at a sunny day.

"Hello," she said.

He turned and she saw the haggard lines on his face, the worry in his eyes. "Hello," he answered softly. "How are you feeling?"

"Okay, I think. A little sore. The baby's okay, too."

Crossing to the bed, he picked up her hand and held it tight in his. "They're still waiting on a couple of tests, but the doctors seem to think everything looks normal so far. You have a slight concussion, some bruising, but no broken bones. Thank God you were in the Mercedes and the air bags worked the way they're supposed to."

She tried to remember but couldn't quite do it. "Was I in an accident?"

"Another car hit you. The police believe the other driver had had one drink too many, but he passed the Breathalyzer, so he was only cited for speeding.

They said you were going a little too fast, as well. You were lucky, Peyton. It could easily have been much worse. Much worse.''

''Hmm.'' She didn't feel alarm or even a great deal of concern. Probably the bliss of medication. Or simply knowing neither she nor the baby had been seriously hurt. ''Why was I driving?'' she asked. ''Do you know?''

''You don't remember driving off and leaving me at the restaurant?''

That sounded vaguely familiar. ''How did you get home?''

''Took a cab.'' He squeezed her hand, looked distraught. ''You scared the life out of me, Peyton. I am never going to argue with you again. Ever.''

''That seems a little drastic, Matt. Some of our arguments have been very…stimulating.''

He sank into the chair, never easing the security of his grip on her hand. ''This one very nearly cost me my wife and daughter.''

''Son,'' she responded automatically. ''And we're both okay, Matt. You can stop looking so despondent. Everything's fine. I'm not going to die. I barely even have a headache. If you keep this up, they'll have to bring a bed in here for you.''

''If it comes to that, I'll just climb into your bed.''

''Now *that* sounds like the man I married.''

He dropped his gaze, brought it back again to

meet hers. "I hoped it might sound a little like the man you love."

Her breath caught at the hope that suddenly blossomed inside her, banishing the ache. "It sounded a *lot* like him, if you want to know the truth."

"It's time for truth between us, Peyton. No more pretending. No more hiding. I'm in love with you. It's been coming on so gradually, I didn't even know it until last night when you told me I'd lost you, too. And then, when I found out you'd been in an accident…" His voice broke and his hold on her hand— and her heart—tightened. "I thought I might have lost you and the baby and I…I knew then that you're all I really care about. You're all that matters. Without you, without the future we backed our way into, I'd have nothing but a sad, lonely life."

She brushed her hand across his unshaven cheek. "You have a wonderful family, Matt. A job you love. And you have me…forever if you want."

A smile tucked into the corners of his mouth. "I want," he said simply. "I love you. I love making love to you. I love that I'm married to you. And I love that we're having a baby. Together."

"That's a lot of love," she said, overcome with emotion. "Luckily, it happens that I feel the same way. You make me happy, Matt. Happier than I ever thought I could be."

He leaned in and pressed a gentle, lingering kiss to her lips. "Ditto. That goes double for me. However, there is one thing I need to clear up. It may change your view of our future."

"Nothing could do that."

He sighed. "I hope you mean that, because the one thing I don't love about my life is my job. You were right when you said if I didn't want to make the tough choices, I should step aside. I should have done it a long time ago. I probably should never have taken the position with the Foundation at all."

"You don't like it?" she asked, realizing that must be the source of his sadness, the reason he felt he was always in danger of disappointing his parents. "Then what are you doing there?"

"Fulfilling my birthright, Peyton. I'm the first-born son of the firstborn son. I'm the Jonathan of my generation. The Foundation is everything to my parents. I thought it was my duty to make it everything to me, as well. It never seemed as if I had a choice."

"Do you have some other career in mind…or are you going to take a little time to think about what you want?"

"Promise you won't laugh, but I've always thought I'd make a good teacher."

She did laugh, but only with happiness. "You'll make a wonderful teacher," she said. "I think that's a great idea. My mother will absolutely hate it."

He grinned. "Maybe she'll come around in time. My parents may not like it much, either."

"Maybe they'll come back and run the Foundation."

"No. I expect Miranda will step in. She's always secretly yearned for the opportunity, I think, and she'll be great at it. Much better than I am."

"I imagine she'll have a lot less trouble dealing with Jessica."

"Which must mean I'll have a lot less trouble with you. If we don't have Jessica to stir up a fuss, what will we find to argue about?"

"Don't worry," Peyton assured him. "We'll think of something."

Raising her hand to his lips, he breathed a sigh of relief into her skin. "Maybe you should sleep on it."

She smiled as she felt the baby move. Taking Matt's hand, she laid it over her stomach and watched with pride and so much love as his eyes widened when he felt the kick.

"Wow," he said. "She's got quite a foot on her."

"Yes," Peyton replied. "He certainly does."

Matt kissed her again. "If it is a boy, we're not naming him Jonathan."

"Hmm," she said. "We'll see." Then she pulled his head down, lured his lips back to hers and lost herself in the sweet taste of happiness.

Epilogue

The wedding took place at dusk on the cliffs behind Danfair.

Hayley wore a simple white dress and carried a bouquet of red peonies. Andrew wore a dark blue tuxedo with a white boutonniere on his lapel, the single flower set into a curlicue of red, white and blue ribbons. Ainsley, in red, was the matron of honor, and Matthew, in traditional black, stood up with his brother as best man.

Afterward the whole family watched the Fourth of July fireworks explode out in the waters beyond Newport Harbor.

Nate and Miranda sat on a blanket behind Will and Cate, who'd both turned their hair a patriotic red, white and blue in honor of the occasion. Not to be outdone, Kali and Kori wore matching sundresses...Kali in red and white, Kori in blue and white…although both had somehow acquired identical grass stains down the front.

Andrew and Hayley, as the day's guests of honor, sat in lawn chairs decorated by Kali and Kori especially for the bride and groom. But it was doubtful the newlyweds saw any fireworks except the ones in each other's eyes.

Ivan sat on the grass, but Ainsley was too excited to be still for long, and she continually popped up to clap and exclaim over an especially colorful fireburst. And as they were all, in her opinion, spectacular, she was on her feet quite a bit.

Matt and Peyton had the whole of a large baby blanket to share between them, so she sat in front, leaning back against him, wrapped in his arms.

Charles and Linney watched from inside the house, deeming the noise and the night too much for their new grandchild, who had arrived on the last day of June, just before midnight, at a healthy seven pounds, eleven ounces.

As it turned out, Matt had been right.

They should have painted the nursery pink.

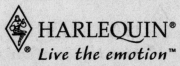

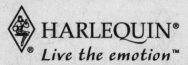

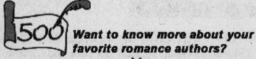

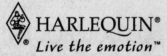

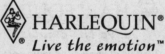

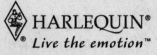

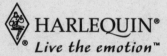